THE ADVENT OF LADY MADELINE

A Novella

PAMELA SHERWOOD

BCP
BLUE CASTLE
PUBLISHING

Published by Blue Castle Publishing

Trade paperback edition/December 2015

Mass-market edition/November 2019

Cover design by Kim Killion

Photograph © staras | Shutterstock.com | Image ID: 206402479

ISBN-13: 978-1-945112-00-3

To my sister, for encouraging me every step of the way,
To Franco Zeffirelli, for the beautiful film version of Romeo and Juliet,
And to whoever invented the drinking game "Never Have I Ever."

"Who chooseth me must give and hazard all he hath."
—WILLIAM SHAKESPEARE, *THE MERCHANT OF VENICE*

Chapter One

How stands your disposition to be married?
—WILLIAM SHAKESPEARE, *Romeo and Juliet*, I, iii

Buckinghamshire, December 1879

"BUT YOU *MUST* GO, HUGO!" Lady Branscombe exhorted her older brother. "Please say that you'll go!"

Hugo Lowell, Viscount Saxby, raised astonished brows. "Charley, my dear—I scarcely know the Whitboroughs. On what pretext could I join their house party?"

"Robert's been invited," she explained. "And he'd be so grateful for your company, especially since *I* can't join him now." She rested a hand upon her rounded abdomen, unmistakable proof that Branscombe's potential heir would be making an appearance within the next three months. "And I do want him to attend. Whitborough's offered him some excellent advice about investments in the past—I should like to see their acquaintance thrive."

Hugo could hardly blame his sister for that wish. Whitborough's business acumen and numerous successful enterprises had earned him the nickname of "The Golden Duke." Fortunate indeed was the man admitted to His Grace's circle of friends and associates.

"And then, there's Wilf," Lady Branscombe continued with a somewhat doom-laden air.

"Wilf? What has our brother to do with this?"

"He's going too—as a guest of Lord Denforth's."

The reason for his sister's misgivings became abundantly clear. Whitborough's eldest son was accounted a young man of great charm and spirit—possibly too much spirit, Hugo mused ruefully. A daring rider, a proficient marksman, and a graceful dancer... who spent money like water and showed an immoderate fondness for games of chance. And the other fashionable young gentlemen drawn into his orbit shared his extravagant tastes. "I thought our Wilf might be a little too young for Denforth's set."

"He's of age now—just. We can't exactly pick and choose his friends for him. But if *you* went to the Whitboroughs—"

"You think *I* might provide a mitigating influence?" Hugo inquired skeptically.

"I know you would! He does look up to you, for all he pretends not to."

"Mm." Hugo drummed his fingers on the arm of the sofa. "You know that I'm promised to Earl Clement's for Christmas?"

His sister did not quite meet his eyes. "I—had heard something of that nature..."

Hugo fixed her with a stern gaze. "Evangeline Charlotte Anne Lowell Branscombe—"

"Oh, very well!" she exclaimed, a touch pettishly. "I know you've been paying court to Lady Althea Clement. But nothing's official yet, is it? You haven't *formally* offered for her?"

The anxious note in her voice surprised him. "No, not yet," he conceded, after a moment. "That is, I am not Lady Althea's only admirer, but I was thinking that Christmas might be the ideal time to—ask her to consider my suit." He regarded his sister narrowly. "You have some objections to the lady who may become the future Countess of Bevington?"

"Oh, no! That is," Lady Branscombe bit her lip, "from all I know of her, Lady Althea is a paragon of virtue and amiability—along with being pretty and well-dowered."

"She is all of those things," Hugo said with no small

satisfaction. He hadn't expected to find so suitable a potential bride this quickly, when he'd only begun his search this past spring.

"Only—she's not likely to stir things up for you, is she?"

"I wasn't aware that things *required* stirring up," he retorted. "At least not where *I'm* concerned! There's much to be said for a quiet life."

"But a quiet life doesn't have to be an uneventful one! Or a—a dull one. I'm not saying that Lady Althea is dull," Lady Branscombe added hastily, though Hugo suspected she *had* been saying just that. "It's just—well, I worry so about you, my dear!"

"Worry about *me*?" he echoed, astonished.

"You're not yet thirty, but you've grown so settled and staid!" his sister lamented. "I know most of it's because of Papa's accident, but I miss the brother who used to climb trees and play pirates or Robin Hood with me!"

Hugo found himself smiling. They'd been a pair, he and Charley, roaming the forests of Nottinghamshire together. She'd always insisted on being Will Scarlet or Allan-a-Dale, wanting to go on adventures rather than stay behind in Sherwood Forest, like Maid Marian. He cherished those memories all the more in light of the responsibilities he'd had to shoulder at sixteen, after their formerly active, vigorous father ended up in an invalid's chair.

"Now the only entertainment you allow yourself is riding to hounds," Lady Branscombe went on. "Or attending the occasional shooting party. Heaven knows I don't begrudge you those, but what about the rest of the year?" She paused, flushing slightly, then resumed, "Try as I might, I cannot imagine Lady Althea... well, she just doesn't seem the adventurous *sort*."

"Not everyone is meant to be," Hugo pointed out. "That shouldn't be a black mark against him—or her."

"Of course not. But I can't help wanting the best for my brother—not merely what the world deems proper or suitable." She bit her lip, gazing at him with wistful eyes. "Forgive me?"

Hugo took her hand, squeezing it affectionately.

"There's nothing to forgive, Charley. I am touched that you desire my happiness so strongly. But there is no reason to suppose I couldn't be happy with Lady Althea, is there? Should she accept my offer, that is."

She squeezed his hand in return, a resigned smile playing about her lips. "Why wouldn't she accept? You're quite the catch, you know. When are the Clements expecting you?"

"I haven't written them yet, but I thought I might go down on the twenty-third."

Her eyes lit up. "Oh, but that's perfect! Robert says the Whitborough house party is due to end on the *twenty-first*. So you could *still* go to the Clements' as planned, and not miss a day!"

"Charley—"

"If you went, it needn't be just to bear Robert company or keep an eye on Wilf. It could be an adventure for *you!*" Lady Branscombe insisted, holding his hand even tighter. "When's the last time you did something new and different? And you could write to me about it—tell me of all the things you've done that you haven't before. It would certainly beguile the time for *me*," she added, gazing ruefully down at herself.

Hugo could feel himself weakening, but he mustered one more protest. "I cannot feel my presence would be all that necessary—"

His sister smiled at him, her brown eyes alight with fond amusement. "A handsome bachelor is always necessary—and welcome—at a country house party! Though you needn't worry about Whitborough's daughters complicating things," she assured him hastily. "Two are still in the schoolroom, and the eldest has turned down every proposal she's received since she came out. I hear she's practically on the shelf—and likes it that way!"

Hugo sighed, capitulating. "You say you want to hear of whatever new and different things I may do? Well, never before have I accepted an invitation at the very last minute, nor attended a house party where I did not know the hosts. So, my dear Charley, that's two for the list already!"

❄

Denforth Castle, Yorkshire, three days later

"I REQUIRE A HUSBAND."

The words rang through the bedchamber like a challenge, and Lady Madeline Lyons pulled a face, relieved that no one was present to hear her make that declaration.

Except for her reflection, which—as a fanciful child—Madeline had named "Mariette" and sometimes pretended was her twin, instead of Hal. Much as she loved her brother, there were times when she'd desperately longed for a sister with whom she could share all her secrets and who would never betray her confidences. A sister who would understand everything that had led her to this moment... and this not wholly palatable realization.

A husband, a home, and perhaps someday a family of her own. She'd vaguely supposed she'd marry one day, but she'd been in no hurry to do so on first coming out. But time—and other matters—had a way of changing one's perspective, she mused, studying "Mariette" in the glass.

No fault to be found there, fortunately. Her green evening gown was becoming and exquisitely cut—French, of course—as well as flattering to her dark coloring. *Maman*'s coloring. The Duchess of Whitborough had an unerring instinct for which styles and hues would suit her and her daughters best. And however they might clash over those... other matters, Madeline willingly yielded to her mother's authority when it came to fashion.

But a beautiful dress wouldn't be the only thing on display. Raising her chin just a fraction, Madeline tried for a smile that was more than the cursory curving of lips she'd perfected as an increasingly bored debutante. A smile that would reach her eyes for a change.

She abandoned the first attempt halfway through. And tried to imagine herself speaking to a man who was interested in something other than her position and her dowry, who might actually *care* about her thoughts and opinions. Experience had shown her that such a man was rare, but there was a remote possibility that he might exist. Somewhere. It would be nothing short of a miracle if he was among those attending this house party, but wasn't Christmas supposed to be the season of miracles?

There. That was a *little* better. A trifle less forced, and she could practice until it felt more natural.

A knock on her door had her turning from the mirror. "Who is it?" she called.

"Just me, Maddie," her sister Elaine replied from the passage. "May I come in?"

"Of course, darling." Madeline smiled at the younger girl as she slipped into the room. After three brothers, it had been lovely to have a sister at last, and despite the six years between them, they'd always got on well.

"I was hoping I could borrow your amethysts to liven up this dress," Elaine explained, gesturing at her pale lavender gown. "My pearls just make it look insipid."

"It definitely could use something more colorful," Madeline agreed. "My jewel box is on the vanity. Help yourself."

"Thanks!" Elaine hurried over to the vanity. "I can't wait to be out of the schoolroom. I'm so tired of wearing white and pastels!"

"You look lovely in them all the same," Madeline said loyally. "Much better than I ever did." Elaine was as fair as she was dark, with tawny-blonde hair, their mother's hazel eyes, and an English rose complexion.

"Well, you look stunning in that shade of green," Elaine remarked, studying her sister's gown a touch enviously.

Madeline smoothed her skirts, trying not to appear self-conscious. "Thank you, Lainey. I just hope you're not the only one who thinks so."

"Oh?" Elaine's brows rose. "Are you speaking of anyone in particular?"

Madeline avoided her gaze. "Not exactly. But—well, I suppose there's no point in beating round the bush. I'll be putting some serious effort into finding a husband, starting with this week's house party!"

"Truly? After all this time—and all those proposals you refused?"

Madeline just managed not to wince. "I know how long it's been! And I don't imagine that those gentlemen cherish fond memories of me, but I did have my reasons for saying 'no.' Besides, can I help it if *Maman* taught me to be—particularly discriminating?"

Elaine dimpled. "You mean picky!".

Madeline narrowed her eyes. "Do you want to borrow my amethysts or not?"

"Sorry," Elaine said hastily, delving back into the jewel box. "Well, if it helps, lots of young men have come for the week," she reported. "At least three of Hal's friends, one of Reg's, and another gentlemen joined the party at virtually the last minute."

"Have any of them ever been here before?"

Elaine paused, Madeline's amethyst pendant dangling from her fingers. "I don't *think* so, but they're bound to be good-looking, aren't they? *And* wealthy. Hal's friends, anyway."

Good-looking, wealthy—and extravagant, Madeline supplied inwardly. Like Hal himself—which was hardly surprising. In all probability, they'd be keen sportsmen, dress well, and show to advantage in a ballroom or salon. But would any of them be good *husband* material?

That remained to be seen—especially since Madeline wasn't sure *Hal* was, despite their parents' plans to formalize *his* betrothal this very week. Still, she couldn't dismiss the possibility out of hand.

"*I'll look to like if looking liking move*," she murmured, half to herself.

Surely among the eligible men attending this house party, there must be one or two she could like. And perhaps something could grow from that.

She glanced over at her sister, now fastening the pendant about her throat. Lainey was a dear and very sympathetic, but she was only sixteen. It would be ages yet before she had to worry about the things consuming Madeline's attention now. Besides, Madeline strongly suspected that there was already a most eligible young man waiting in the wings for Elaine, even if nothing had been officially arranged. As recently as three months ago, Madeline would have recoiled from the very idea of having one's marital prospects settled so early. Now, it seemed almost... comforting, to have such a certainty to fall back on.

A pounding on the door cut into her ruminations. "Maddie! Are you in there? Please, I need your help!"

Their younger sister Juliana's voice, edged with something very like panic. Exchanging an alarmed glance with Elaine, Madeline responded at once. "Yes, I'm here, Ju! Come in."

The door burst open and the girl practically hurtled into the room, her frock rumpled and her red-gold hair escaping from its plaits.

"Darling, what's wrong?" Madeline asked.

"It's Volumnia! I can't find her *anywhere!*"

Relaxing, Madeline shook her head indulgently. "She's a *cat*, Ju. She'll turn up when she wants to be found, which will most likely be when she's hungry."

"You don't understand, Maddie! She could have kittens any day now." Juliana wrung her hands, her blue eyes huge with distress. "Miss Withersedge won't have her in the nursery. She told me to put Volumnia in the stables, but that's much too cold for her, and she's never been outside the castle. I made a nest for her in the west attic, but she must have got out somehow, because she's gone!"

"Oh, Lord!" That definitely put a new complexion on the matter. "Any idea how long she's been missing?"

Juliana bit her lip. "An hour? Maybe two?"

Madeline stifled a most unladylike exclamation. Dear heaven, the wretched animal could be anywhere! Denforth's tribe of assorted felines had the run of the castle, but a heavily pregnant cat was *not* the sort of thing one wished to lose sight of in a houseful of guests—especially young men one was hoping to impress!

Rising, Elaine glanced at the mantel clock. "There's still a little time before dinner, Ju," she said consolingly. "Perhaps we can go and look for her. She might not have gone *too* far in her—present condition."

Madeline opened her mouth to protest, but softened when she saw Juliana's eyes brighten hopefully. "Oh, very well," she conceded, sighing. "I suppose she could have gone to ground in a cupboard or closet."

Or a guest chamber. Suppressing a shudder at the thought, she inquired briskly, "Now, is Volumnia the tabby or the tortoiseshell?"

"WELL, there's no need to get huffy about it, Ger!" Madeline exclaimed, as her younger brother's door closed most emphatically in her face.

"He wouldn't *really* do it, would he, Maddie?" Juliana whispered to her sister.

"Yes, I would!" Gervase retorted, on the other side of the door.

Madeline rolled her eyes and led Juliana away. "No, sweeting, I'm sure that he *wouldn't*," she said, once they were out of earshot. "Though you can't really blame him for saying so, under the circumstances. Just as well Volumnia didn't choose *his* room this time."

She turned to survey the remaining doors before them. Agreeing that they could cover more ground separately, the sisters had headed in opposite directions, Elaine hurrying off to check the north section of the wing, while Madeline and Juliana took the south.

The first order of business had been to make sure Volumnia hadn't intruded upon the guests. Fortunately, none of them had reported seeing her, and most had been tolerant of the sisters' search and solicitous about the expectant mother—Gervase excepted.

"Do you think Volumnia might have gone to Margaret's room?" Juliana suggested hopefully. "*She* likes cats."

"So she does." Their friend and neighbor Lady Margaret Carlisle was nothing if not good-humored, a quality that endeared her to many in the Lyons family. "She and Alicia are sharing the Rose Room. We'll try there next."

"Ladies, if I may have your attention?" a resonant male voice inquired.

Madeline turned... and abruptly found herself lost for words.

Two doors down, leaning against the jamb, stood a man who could have modeled as one of the heroes of the *Iliad*. Not Achilles or Paris, her mind supplied dazedly. This was the noble Hector: tall, deep-chested, and broad-shouldered. Fair curling hair, eyes the light golden-brown of acorns, even features in an undeniably handsome face...

The gentleman smiled, a touch wryly, but it did not detract from the good humor she saw in his eyes. "Viscount Saxby, at your service." He sketched them a bow. "I believe I can assist you in your quest."

Chapter Two

Some men there are love not a gaping pig;
Some, that are mad, if they behold a cat...
—WILLIAM SHAKESPEARE, *The Merchant of*
  Venice, IV, i

"*THERE YOU ARE!*" Lady Juliana Lyons exclaimed thank-fully, as she lifted up the skirts of the counterpane. "Here, puss, puss, puss..."

The front half of her vanished under Hugo's bed, then emerged some moments later, clutching a squirming tortoiseshell cat to her chest.

"She must have got in while my valet was bringing in my trunks," Hugo remarked to the tall, dark-haired Lady Madeline Lyons, who was regarding her sister and the cat with mingled relief and exasperation. "And then slipped under the bed unnoticed. *I* didn't notice, until I sat down on the bed myself and heard her cry out. It was —a most extraordinary sound."

Lady Madeline's lips twitched into a reluctant smile. "It is indeed. I hope you weren't too startled, Lord Saxby."

"Not in the least," Hugo assured her. He certainly wasn't about to tell his host's lovely daughters that he'd all but jumped out of his skin on hearing that piercing caterwaul.

"Thank you so much, Lord Saxby," Lady Juliana said

breathlessly, scrambling to her feet. "I'm sorry Volumnia's been such a nuisance. But she's only like this because she's going to have kittens!"

Good God! Hugo eyed the cat with fresh alarm, noticing that she was indeed noticeably *enceinte*. Even further along than Charley was. He doubted that his sister would appreciate the comparison. "Er, is the blessed event due to occur soon?"

Lady Juliana regarded the cat critically. "I can't be sure. Maybe in the next day or so?"

"As long as it's not in anyone else's chamber! She had her last litter in our brother Gervase's bed," Lady Madeline explained to Hugo. "He expressed himself—rather forcefully about it, then and now."

"He threatened to turn her into a muff," Lady Juliana reported with a giggle, cuddling her pet close. "And to do the skinning himself."

Hugo felt a decided twinge of sympathy for Lord Gervase. The beast—*Volumnia?*—made a baleful sound between a mew and a growl that her mistress ignored.

"Well, now that you've got her, Ju, we should be on our way," Lady Madeline said, rather pointedly. She turned to Hugo. "Thank you, Lord Saxby, for your assistance. We apologize for disturbing you."

"Not at all. I was glad to be of help." He paused, then surprised himself by inquiring, "I shall see you at dinner, then, Lady Madeline?"

Her eyes widened fractionally. "Yes, at dinner. Good evening, my lord." She ushered herself and her sister out of his room.

Hugo closed the door, leaned against it bemusedly. Barely two hours since his arrival at Denforth Castle, and things were already proving more—eventful than he was accustomed to. Not in a *bad* way, though he hoped the rest of the family livestock weren't in the habit of invading the guest chambers!

Although it was almost worth the trouble, he mused, if it brought such enchanting visitors as the Lyons sisters to his door. Lady Juliana looked no older than twelve, but she was already a charmer, with that bright hair and those sparkling blue eyes. No doubt she'd have suitors by the dozen when she made her debut and started thinking about young men instead of cats.

Lady Madeline's looks were equally striking, though she was a very different type from her sister. More like her mother the Duchess, whom Hugo had finally met on his arrival: the same dark hair, fine bones, and ivory complexion—even the same air of self-possession. But while Her Grace's eyes were hazel, Lady Madeline's were closer to green. Perhaps with a touch of blue, Hugo mused, remembering his first good view of them. Or grey.

Changeable eyes. Sea-colored eyes. Lady Althea had blue eyes—light and pretty as a spring sky. He could not recall them being any other color but blue.

Not that there was anything wrong with that, he told himself hastily. Blue eyes were lovely and—in Lady Althea's case—made a perfect match with her butter-blonde hair and pink-and-white complexion. Just what one would expect in an English rose.

He ignored the voice in his head that insinuated that the *unexpected* could be lovely too. And that English roses were *not* the only flowers in the garden. Pushing that traitorous thought aside, he summoned Gibson to help him dress for dinner.

"LORD SAXBY WAS AWFULLY nice about all this," Juliana remarked as she and Madeline headed back the way they had come. She tightened her hold on Volumnia, who grumbled but made no attempt to free herself from the girl's grasp.

"He was indeed." Which spoke well of him, Madeline reflected. Not everyone was as tolerant of finding strange animals under their beds. And his expression while watching Juliana had been quite indulgent. Had he younger siblings of his own, perhaps?

She racked her brain, trying to remember anything she might have heard about him or his family and wishing she'd paid more attention when *Maman* had been compiling the guest list. The answers to some of her questions might lie in Debrett's but she'd no time to consult it before dinner. At least she'd have a chance to see and perhaps speak with the charming viscount then. And if she were very fortunate, he might even be seated beside her.

Her pulse quickened at the thought. Something else she had in common with *Maman*: an appreciation for a handsome man, which Lord Saxby most certainly was. Elaine might have teased her about being picky, but it had been a while since a man had made such a strong impression upon her—possibly not since her first Season. She'd been out five years now: how was it that they had not met before?

Lord Saxby must be at least a few years older than Hal and his friends. She would have placed his age at just under thirty, and Madeline had turned twenty-three this past summer. No longer a young girl, but that was all to the good as far as she was concerned. She knew herself to be much more poised and confident now than she'd been at eighteen—all the better to hold the attention of a mature man.

She mustn't rush things, however. First impressions were important—but further acquaintance was essential, to judge the *depth* of an attraction properly. Still, Madeline reasoned, a gentleman as good-natured as he was good-looking was worth cultivating... if she could just be certain that there was no *Lady* Saxby in the picture or in the offing.

"—stay with you?"

Juliana's voice broke into her thoughts, and Madeline started to utter an absent-minded agreement, but stopped short as the realization of what her sister was asking sank in. "Ju, for heaven's sake!"

"Please, Maddie!" her sister implored, her eyes huge and beseeching over the cat in her arms. "You *know* I can't take Volumnia back to the nursery! And I *won't* take her out to the stables, and she's already got out of the attic! Can't she stay in your room, *just* for tonight? I'll find another place for her tomorrow, I promise!"

Volumnia made a pitiful sound, and once again, Madeline found herself weakening. She was fond enough of cats, and it wasn't the animal's fault that she'd got in the family way. Besides, it was the Christmas season, she reflected, a touch wryly. What better time to show charity towards expectant mothers?

"One night," she conceded at last, bending a stern gaze upon Juliana. "We'll find a basket for her, and she can sleep in my dressing room. But tomorrow, she stays elsewhere!"

MOST ESTATES HAD DRAWING ROOMS; Denforth Castle had a Great Hall, in which a fair number of guests had already assembled by the time Hugo entered.

The first person he recognized was Branscombe, who beckoned to him with a smile. Relieved, Hugo made his way over the fireplace, where his brother-in-law was standing.

"Glad to see you didn't get lost on the way," Branscombe remarked jovially, clapping him on the shoulder.

"It was a close-run thing," Hugo admitted, "but one of the footmen pointed me in the right direction."

"Excellent. I've heard Her Grace has the staff at Denforth running like clockwork."

She'd have to, in an establishment this size, Hugo reflected, especially with a house party in residence. Branscombe had said there would be at least twenty people attending, not counting the family. Aloud he remarked, "I know you told me who was who while we were on the train, but it's going to take some time for me to match all the names with the faces."

"I'll point them out to you, then, as discreetly as possible. Although," Branscombe added with a hint of a smirk, "I trust you'll have no trouble recognizing our hosts?"

"None whatsoever." Their Graces were nothing if not distinctive. "*And* I've met Denforth a time or two," he added, reminded once more of the young earl's potentially undesirable influence on Wilf.

Fortunately, his younger brother *hadn't* gone into a sulk at the news that Hugo would be attending the Whitborough house party, though he had made a point of avoiding him and Branscombe at the train station, saying that he was already sharing a compartment with friends. In keeping with his promise to Charley, Hugo supposed he should observe which of Denforth's other companions were present and whether Wilf was following their example too closely.

"Well, over there is his next youngest brother, Lord Reginald," Branscombe began, indicating a tall, blond young man with an almost military bearing. "Destined for the army, I understand, and already looking every inch a soldier."

He did indeed, Hugo mused, right down to the thousand-yard stare and the stern, uncompromising jut of his jaw. Lord Reginald and Denforth both favored their father, with their fair coloring and athletic builds. But there was something... harder about the younger man, a sharper, keener edge that was missing from his elder brother, whom Hugo now spotted striding into the Great Hall, his smile almost as bright as his hair. Several of the ladies present turned their faces towards him like flowers following the progress of the sun. He *did* have charisma, Hugo conceded grudgingly. But charisma did not necessarily indicate strength of character.

He was even less pleased at the sight of the two young men entering on Denforth's heels: Lord Rupert Bonham and the Honorable Clarence Moresby. Handsome enough in their way, if lacking Denforth's glamour, but every bit as idle and spendthrift as their leader. Lord Rupert, especially: he was the second son of the Marquess of Wyndross, Hugo remembered. A darkly handsome fellow whose liking for sport was as keen as Hugo's own, though he'd also a taste for certain... town pleasures that Hugo did not share. Indeed, Hugo had heard that Bonham was something of a rake.

Frowning, he scanned the swelling assembly of guests for Wilf, not knowing whether to be relieved or anxious that his brother hadn't entered with the rest of Denforth's set.

"—Lord Gervase Lyons." Branscombe's voice interrupted his thoughts. "He doesn't resemble his brothers, but I've heard he's quite clever. Just went up to Oxford this Michaelmas."

Hurriedly, Hugo glanced in the direction his brother-in-law had indicated. This must be the same Lord Gervase who'd objected so strenuously to a cat having kittens in his bed, and small blame to him. He looked to be about nineteen or twenty, browner and more lightly built than his brothers, but his gaze was as keen and assessing as a man's twice his age.

"And that's the Duke of Castlebrooke he's talking to," Branscombe went on. "They're much of an age, I understand, and attending the same college."

"Really?" Hugo took a closer look at the auburn-haired youth standing next to Lord Gervase. "I'd no idea we were in such exalted company—*two* dukes at a house party."

"Three," Branscombe corrected. "Their Graces of Langdale are here as well. They're old friends of the Whitboroughs, practically neighbors in fact." He nodded towards a pleasant-looking middle-aged couple, flanked by a girl of perhaps seventeen and a youth a few years younger. "And those are their two eldest children: Lady Margaret Carlisle and Lord Harrowfield. The youngest, Lady Alicia, is still in the schoolroom."

Hugo hummed an absent-minded acknowledgment. Wilf had just come into the Great Hall and was glancing about him uncertainly. Hugo suppressed the urge to beckon or even wave, knowing that his brother would most likely resent what he perceived as interference, and watched resignedly as Wilf spied Denforth's set and made his way over to them.

"—Middletons, Sir George and his family," Branscombe went on. "Also friends and neighbors of the Whitboroughs, though at slightly closer remove. Sir George is the local M.F.H. I'm sure you'll want to make *his* acquaintance as soon as possible!"

He wasn't wrong. Ordinarily, Hugo *would* have been eager to know more about Middleton, the pack he ran, and the country in which they'd be hunting. But a flash of color had drawn his eye to the doorway where two young women currently stood, looking like an exquisite portrait study in contrasts: a dainty blonde in lavender, who looked about sixteen, and willowy, dark-haired Lady Madeline in green. The very best of light and dark, Hugo found himself thinking.

Suddenly, as though she could hear those thoughts, Lady Madeline turned her head, her sea-colored eyes meeting his own from across the room. Good Lord, had she actually been *looking* for him?

Don't flatter yourself, old boy, Hugo told himself. Most likely, Lady Madeline was ascertaining that he was in a good humor and not holding a grudge because of his feline visitor. Under the circumstances, it seemed only right to send her a small, reassuring smile.

Lady Madeline's eyes widened at that, then her lips curved in an answering smile that sent an unexpected jolt through him. Her face was lovely in repose, but the smile enhanced that loveliness, imparting warmth and humor to features that might otherwise seem remote in their almost classical symmetry. A woman instead of a goddess... and Hugo had always preferred the former to the latter.

On impulse, he closed his left eye in the briefest of winks—and thought he saw the faintest flush warm Lady Madeline's ivory skin, but she did not appear offended. Even more tellingly, she did not look away.

"Ah, and there are Whitborough's two eldest daughters," Branscombe spoke up again, beside him. "Lady Madeline and Lady Elaine. Pretty girls, aren't they?"

"Very," Hugo agreed, though he privately thought that "pretty" was almost too tame a word for Lady Madeline's distinctive looks. "I've already met the elder daughter—briefly," he added, surprising himself with the admission.

"Indeed?" Much to Hugo's relief, his brother-in-law sounded only mildly interested; Charley, by contrast, would have seized upon such a tidbit—and imbued it with far more significance than it merited. "I've encountered her just a handful of times myself. Mostly at parties—she's been out for several years, but with her advantages, I suppose she feels no great compulsion to marry."

Charley had said something similar, Hugo recalled, but he couldn't help wondering if Lady Madeline's parents had anything to do with her decision. Just then, as though conjured by his thoughts, the Whitboroughs entered the Great Hall. No denying they made a striking pair, he mused: the duchess with her dark beauty and exquisite bones, the duke no less splendid, in an almost leonine way, with piercing sapphire-blue eyes and a full head of tawny hair, barely touched with grey. Even more compelling was the sense of power they wore so comfortably, like matching cloaks. One could easily imagine they would be most exacting, when it came to approving suitors for their eldest daughter's hand. Perhaps they'd even scared off a few? A pity if it were so: a prize like Lady Madeline was surely worth the hazard.

Not that it was any of *his* affair, Hugo reminded himself hastily. He'd matrimonial plans of his own, and once this house party was over, he'd have the time and opportunity to pursue them. So he let his gaze drift about the room, noting the other guests and absorbing Branscombe's further comments in silence.

And when Her Grace approached him some minutes later, he was not—most assuredly *not*—disappointed to learn that he would be escorting Miss Christabel Middleton, rather than Lady Madeline!

GIVEN THE ORDER OF PRECEDENCE, Madeline was not surprised to find herself paired with Lord Rupert Bonham at dinner. He was a marquess's son, after all, and blessed with a handsome allowance and an even more handsome face. Most eligible, if one went by appearances alone.

She believed she had his measure before the fish course was over: witty, amusing, agreeable in an indolent sort of way, but no more mature than Hal was, really, despite being a few years older than her twin. Ripe for any flirtation, she had no doubt, but she suspected the very mention of anything more serious would cause Lord Rupert to blench and hastily find reason to be elsewhere. Nonetheless, she could enjoy his practiced gallantries on a superficial level through the meal, even though her thoughts and glances kept straying towards another man.

Viscount Saxby was seated on the opposite side of the table, beside eighteen-year-old Christabel Middleton, who was accounted the beauty of her family. Madeline found Olivia, the elder Middleton daughter, much more interesting; however, she wasn't a susceptible young man. She was secretly pleased to note that Lord Saxby did not appear to be particularly captivated by his companion, though his demeanor remained as pleasant as ever.

A good-humored, good-natured man, she mused, remembering the smile and wink he'd given her in the Great Hall. And a patient one: would any other man—

Lord Rupert, for example—have been as tolerant of Volumnia's presence in his chamber and of Juliana's efforts to retrieve her? Madeline doubted it.

Was it because Saxby was an eldest child himself? She'd managed to glean that much from her mother, before dinner; his younger brother, the Honorable Wilfred Lowell, was also present at this house party, as one of Hal's boon companions. A lanky youth with the same fair coloring as his brother, but without the easy confidence and self-assurance. Still growing into himself, a boy just becoming a man, much like Madeline's own brothers—and she included Hal in that assessment, twin or no. Indeed, there were times when the ten minutes that separated her birth from his felt like ten *years*.

Lord Saxby must be a good five or six years older than the Honorable Wilfred, so perhaps he'd had ample time to learn patience. And kindness, which was a quality Madeline had come to value over the years—not least because it wasn't the most salient trait in her own family, especially among her parents and brothers!

Still, Madeline reminded herself, she couldn't form a complete opinion of the viscount's character on a single encounter, any more than she could take something as ephemeral as a wink or a smile as evidence of interest on *his* part. She'd more sense than that—she hoped. But this house party should give her the opportunity to get to know him better. *And* the other young men as well, she conceded in the interests of fairness. Perhaps even Lord Rupert had sterling qualities of which she was yet unaware. Resolutely, she turned back to smile at whatever he had just said.

DINNER WAS EXCELLENT, as befitted the house and the season. Hugo suspected that the Duchess of Whitborough, being half-French, was responsible for the array of Continental dishes that found their way onto the table. She was almost certainly responsible for the excellent wines that accompanied each course—the estate of her father, the late Comte de Sevigny, had boasted a fine expanse of vineyards.

The only thing about the meal that Hugo didn't

enjoy was the sight of Lord Rupert Bonham ogling Lady Madeline as though she were one of the morsels on his plate. Fortunately, the lady appeared unbeguiled. After all, Hugo reasoned, as Whitborough's eldest daughter, she could do a good deal better for herself than an idle rake like Lord Rupert! Relieved, he addressed himself to his own plate and, occasionally, Miss Christabel Middleton, who was very pretty but hadn't much to say for herself.

According to custom, the ladies departed after the last course, leaving the men to their port and cigars. Sipping at a glass of as fine a port as a man could desire, Hugo allowed himself to relax fully for the first time since his arrival. While he enjoyed the company of women, he'd always felt most at home among men, especially those who shared his interest in sport.

Not surprisingly, the conversations swirling around him centered on the next morning's hunt, the weather, the terrain—on which Sir George Middleton was happy to expound, and the merits of everyone's respective horses. Some of the younger men were apt to be competitive when it came to the last—Denforth and Lord Reginald, in particular. Such talk was common enough among sportsmen, but their increasingly heated exchanges made Hugo uneasy. He was not unfamiliar with sibling rivalry, but this felt as though it were in an entirely different class. Fortunately, before the brothers' boasting could escalate into an outright quarrel, Whitborough suggested that the men join the ladies in the Great Hall.

The rest of the evening passed agreeably enough, with music about the piano. Lady Madeline played—competently, if not brilliantly—to accompany Lady Elaine, who sang a few traditional airs in a clear, sweet soprano. Everyone joined in on a selection of popular songs from *H.M.S Pinafore*, then retired to their chambers in anticipation of an early rise.

Mellowed by food and wine, Hugo went up the stairs at an unhurried pace, content to let others precede him. Reaching the second floor landing, he was surprised to find Lady Madeline standing there, ostensibly examining her hem as though for loose stitches. As he approached, she straightened up and smiled at him.

"Good evening, Lord Saxby."

"Good evening, Lady Madeline," Hugo returned. The thought that she might have been waiting for *him* crossed his mind, but he dismissed it at once as absurd, even conceited.

"I hope you are finding Denforth to your liking. Despite the earlier—intrusion," she added, a charming mixture of amusement and apology in her tone.

Hugo relaxed, smiling back. "Thank you, Lady Madeline. I'm quite comfortable here, and I trust my recent visitor is, as well?"

"She should be. Juliana persuaded me to allow Volumnia to sleep in my dressing room for the night. I still can't figure out how," she added, shaking her head bemusedly.

"Younger sisters—younger siblings, in general, have a way of wrapping one about their little fingers," he pointed out.

Her lips quirked in a rueful smile. "So they do! Have you other siblings besides your brother, Lord Saxby?"

"Two sisters, both married now. Wilf is the youngest in our family. Is Lady Juliana the youngest in yours?"

"Second youngest. My brother Jason comes after her —he's almost ten." Her changeable eyes sparked with amusement. "To quote Wordsworth's poem, '*We are seven.*'"

"Quite a brood," Hugo remarked as they headed along the passage towards their chambers. "But you seem quite close—at least you and your sisters do," he qualified, remembering the odd tension between Denforth and Lord Reginald.

"Oh, I wanted sisters for the longest time," she confessed. "I was the only girl for almost seven *years,* so I couldn't have been happier when Lainey and then Ju were born."

"Maddie!"

A slight figure in a white nightgown was running towards them, plaits streaming behind her like twin banners. Even in the dimly lit passage, Hugo recognized Lady Juliana's bright head.

"It's Volumnia!" the girl exclaimed, skidding to a stop before them. "She's having the kittens *now!*"

"*Now?*" Lady Madeline echoed, paling visibly. For a

moment, Hugo wondered if she were about to have a fit of the vapors—not that he would have blamed her. "In my dressing room? Oh, Lord..." She bit her lip, visibly torn between laughter and annoyance. "Nothing like a cat for the *worst* possible timing!"

"Four have already been born," Lady Juliana rushed on excitedly. "And your maid—Albertine—says there may be at least two more on the way!"

Her sister winced. "Remind me to double Albertine's salary."

"Would *you* like to come and see the kittens, Lord Saxby?" Lady Juliana asked, looking up at Hugo with those impossibly blue eyes.

"I'm sure Volumnia has matters well in hand, Ju," Lady Madeline interposed, fixing her sister with a stern gaze. "This isn't her first litter, after all."

"But, Maddie—"

"I would be happy to look in for a moment," Hugo broke in. "If you think it won't disturb the new mother. *And* if it's all right with your sister, seeing that it's her dressing room," he added.

Lady Madeline threw him a grateful glance before capitulating with an exasperated sigh. "Oh very well! Let us *all* go, then!"

THE TRAVAIL WAS OVER. Hugo was relieved not to have witnessed the grislier parts, but he duly admired Volumnia's newborn progeny, their eyes still closed, rooting insistently at their mother's now-flaccid belly.

"Two black, two tortoiseshell, one grey, one ginger," Lady Madeline observed, regarding the litter with an expression of wry indulgence. "A full complement of colors. Any idea who the sire might be, Ju?"

"Probably Titus. She and Xerxes can't abide each other." Lady Juliana glanced up from the basket over which she'd been hovering. "Would *you* like to take one of the kittens, Lord Saxby—when they're old enough?"

"Thank you, but I fear I must decline," Hugo replied. "Cats make my mother sneeze."

"Oh, that's too bad!" she sympathized. "But if you were to have your own household—"

"That will do, Juliana," Lady Madeline interrupted. "Doubtless there will be plenty of others eager to adopt a kitten. Margaret might like one, and perhaps Olivia Middleton as well."

"Quite right," Hugo said heartily. "I'm sure you'll have no trouble finding homes for such winsome little chaps, especially once their eyes are open."

Strangely enough, he found that he meant it. While he generally preferred dogs to cats, there was something rather endearing about these squirming, squeaking balls of fur—though he was also grateful that they hadn't made their first appearance in his chamber!

Smiling, Lady Juliana turned back to the basket. Hugo met Lady Madeline's resigned, ruefully amused gaze over her sister's bowed head, while a letter to *his* sister began to compose itself in his mind.

My Dear Charley: Never before have I attended a cat's confinement...

Chapter Three

AT LEAST HER habit still fit. Madeline regarded her reflection critically, but the line of the bodice was snug, the drape of the skirt smooth. And the black broadcloth had been excellently cared for, showing no sign of wear. Belatedly, it occurred to her that she might have commissioned another during the Little Season—perhaps in green, to bring out the color of her eyes—but there was no point in dwelling on that oversight.

Leaving the mirror, she went to the window and looked out. No rain or snow, but a feeble sun, just visible through the mists, which would most likely burn off by afternoon. Nothing that would deter avid sportsmen from their pursuit of a fox.

Madeline sighed. While she knew herself to be a good horsewoman and well able to keep up with the rest of the field if she chose, she'd never been the most enthusiastic of hunters. But almost all of the men would be riding out this morning—including Lord Saxby, whom she'd discovered was quite passionate about sport.

She picked up her riding crop and went downstairs.

Breakfast on a hunt morning tended to be a hurried, catch-as-catch-can affair, but Elaine, Margaret, and the Middleton sisters were all in the breakfast parlor, tucking into the food. Joining them, Madeline downed a quick meal of toast, fried ham, and coffee, then headed out to the courtyard with the others.

The sun was shining with slightly more conviction now, illuminating the hunters' scarlet coats—Madeline flatly refused to call them "pink"—and the horses' glossy hides. Sir George's pack was milling about the courtyard as well, eagerly sniffing the air and wagging their tails.

Most of the men were already mounted, Madeline noticed. All her brothers, except Jason, who was probably watching from the nursery window. Hal and Reg sat erect on their respective mounts, deliberately facing away from each other, while Gervase surveyed them both with a sardonic glint in his eyes. And Father, astride Kingmaker, his best hunter...

Madeline felt the familiar ache deep in her chest, of mingled love and resentment. How often she'd seen him like this when she was a child: mounted on his horse and blazing with a vitality that made other men appear like shadows beside him! Sometimes her mother had ridden out with him, though less frequently as their family grew. And the child-Madeline had looked on in something close to awe, marveling that two such splendid people could be *her* parents.

That sort of bedazzlement was destined to end, she supposed. Discovering—and accepting—that one's parents had feet of clay was surely part of growing up. She just hadn't expected that realization to carry such... bitterness with it.

She glanced back towards the steps where *Maman* was standing, beside her dear friend, the Duchess of Langdale. No sign of temper on her mother's exquisitely boned face: on the contrary, she was smiling as she surveyed the company. Madeline fancied she could see the warmth in Her Grace's eyes, especially when her gaze rested on Reg, who had always been her favorite child. And when the Duke looked back at his wife and touched the brim of his hat, he received a cordial nod in response.

Madeline turned away, feeling like an intruder on

such intimacy. After everything her father had done, she still couldn't understand how her mother could have agreed to reconcile with him. But then, it hadn't been her choice to make, the Duchess had pointed out astringently when the subject had arisen between them. Still, that didn't mean Madeline had to *like* it, or live with it.

A handsome bay gelding crossed her field of vision, but it was his rider who caught—and held—her attention. Enough to make any woman's mouth water: Lord Saxby in a black Melton coat that defined his broad shoulders, buff breeches that hugged his splendid thighs, while overhead the strengthening sunlight brightened his hair to gold. *Here's metal more attractive...*

A groom approached, leading Juno, Madeline's favorite mare, and she hastened to mount up, her spirits lifting as she settled into the sidesaddle. Hunting might not be her favorite activity, but the sight of Lord Saxby in riding dress provided ample compensation!

REINING in his horse (an excellent beast), Hugo blotted his forehead and looked around him, breathless, exhilarated, and unable to stop the grin he could feel spreading across his face.

Less than an hour into the hunt, the pack had drawn a fox, who'd led them a merry chase over hedge and field before going to ground somewhere. But to judge from the way Middleton's hounds still sniffed the air and whined, it was possible that he hadn't gone far.

Glancing at his nearest companions, who just happened to be Denforth and Lord Reginald, Hugo saw on their faces the same mixture of excitement and impatience that he was feeling. Caught up in the thrill of the chase and in no hurry for the day's sport to end. Every second seemed an eternity—then, a hound gave voice, and the huntsman's shout of "View halloo!" sent excitement rippling through the crowd like an electric current.

Galvanized, the hunters sprang into action once more. Daring riders that they were, Denforth and Lord Reginald raced immediately towards the front of the pack. So, a little to Hugo's surprise, did Whitborough himself. Granted, the duke was vigorous for a man of his years, but his willingness to take risks when he must be close to fifty was as alarming as it was impressive. Hugo felt a sudden sharp pang when he thought of his own father, who was not much older than Whitborough and had once ridden with equal verve and daring.

He swallowed down the sadness and focused instead on the moment, the wind stinging the blood into his cheeks, the galloping stride of the horse beneath him, the baying of the hounds and the pounding thunder of hooves in his ears. Dear God, could there be anything more exciting than *this*?

Someone was coming up behind him on the left, closing the gap between them. Well and good: Hugo had never minded pacing himself against another rider. More companionable that way, sometimes—

"Oof!"

The oncoming horse shouldered into Hugo's bay, sending the latter staggering sideways into some low-lying brush. Fighting to control his mount *and* keep his seat, Hugo turned a furious glare on the offender. He had the fleeting impression of a hard-featured, florid face set in determined lines and a rawboned, iron-grey hunter who looked every bit as stubborn and uncompromising as his master before the pair swept past him, without so much as an apology or even a perfunctory "pardon me."

Swearing inwardly, Hugo brought his own horse under control, gentling him with hands and words. Much to his relief, the bay didn't seem to have suffered any injuries—no thanks to the grey and his rider. He walked the horse in a slow circle, to calm them both, then prepared to rejoin the hunt.

He couldn't have gone more than half a dozen strides when he heard a woman scream.

Centuries of breeding nudged Hugo in the ribs. With no more than a fleeting moment of regret for the fox, he reined in the bay and headed towards the sound.

He found the source, not at a fence or a hedge, as he'd half-expected but on the banks of a stream, where four wet, bedraggled riders and their horses were straggling ashore. To Hugo's alarm, Wilf was among them—along with Lady Madeline. It took him a moment to recognize the other two as Miss Christabel Middleton and

Lady Margaret Carlisle, the latter on foot and leaning wearily against her mount.

"Good God!" he exclaimed, dismounting at once to assist them. "What happened here? Is anyone hurt?"

Lady Madeline, also on foot, looked up at his approach. "Fortunately, no. But thank you for inquiring, Lord Saxby."

Hugo exhaled, relief washing over him. "I heard the scream and feared the worst."

"That was me," Miss Christabel confessed, looking abashed. "It was the shock, you see! I'm not usually so panicky!"

"My fault!" Wilf broke in, flushing. "Forgive me, Miss Christabel! I didn't mean to crowd you!"

"No need to apologize, Mr. Lowell," she assured him. "I'm quite unharmed—poor Margaret and Madeline may have got the worst of it!"

"And *you* at least rode like a gentleman," Lady Madeline added.

Wilf shook his head, still contrite. "That great pig of a horse—"

"Was it a grey?" Hugo interrupted. "With a hard-faced, middle-aged chap in the saddle?"

"Yes, but how did you—"

"He rode over *me* just before encountering you, from the sound of it." Hugo paused, then said more warmly, "I'm glad to see you're all right, Wilf."

His brother hesitated, then gave him a small smile as Lady Madeline resumed, "We were crossing the stream together, when *he* bulled his way through our midst and knocked us all abroad like a row of dominoes. We're lucky no one *was* hurt—and he didn't stop to inquire about our welfare either."

Wilf blew out a breath. "Who *was* that blighter anyway?"

"Otis Scorton," Miss Christabel replied. "He's a neighbor of ours. Papa doesn't like him much, but he's still a member of the hunt, so we can hardly forbid him to go out with us."

"Hard-riding, hard-drinking, hard-bitten," Lady Madeline summarized, her crisp tones conveying the full extent of her annoyance. "With a mousy wife, a mousier daughter, and two sons who'll probably grow up to be just like him. Fortunately, neither's shown much taste for hunting, so far."

"One unsportsmanlike rider in the family is more than enough," Hugo agreed.

"I say!" Wilf exclaimed, peering ahead of them. "Who's that coming back to us?"

Not Mr. Scorton, Hugo ascertained: the approaching horse was a bay, like his own, only with black stockings and a lighter build—not unlike that of the rider who swung lithely down from the saddle and strode towards them.

"What are *you* doing here, Ger?" Lady Madeline inquired of her brother. "I thought you'd be miles ahead!"

"I turned back when I heard the scream. I thought someone might have come-a-cropper." His grey gaze swept over them—cool but genuinely concerned, Hugo thought.

"Not as bad as that," his sister assured him and quickly supplied the relevant details. "Otis Scorton is in all our black books, however," she concluded, her fine eyes hardening.

"As he should be." Lord Gervase looked them over again. "So everyone is well, I trust? No need for a hurdle?" His eyes sharpened when Lady Margaret failed to stifle a sneeze. "Or a blanket and a hot drink? You all look rather... damp."

"*I'm* all right," Miss Christabel said staunchly. "*And* ready to rejoin the hunt! It'll take more than a bit of water and the likes of Mr. Scorton to keep a Middleton from the field!"

"That's the spirit!" Wilf regarded her with frank admiration. "Well, if you're up for it, Miss Christabel, then so am I! May I—ride with you?"

She dimpled at him. "I should be glad of the company, Mr. Lowell! If you'll excuse us," she added to the others, "we've a fox to catch! And I hope to see you *all* there at the end!"

She touched her heel to her hunter's flank and rode off, Wilf beside her, both picking up the pace as they left the stream behind them.

"Tally-ho," Lord Gervase remarked dryly. "Does that hold for the rest of you as well?"

"Decidedly not! *I've* had enough—and so has Juno!"

Lady Madeline declared, grimacing as she shook out the damp skirts of her habit. The mare was winded, its sides heaving, and she stroked its nose soothingly. "I'm for home, a bath, and a cup of tea!"

"Very sensible." Lord Gervase turned to the bedraggled Lady Margaret, who was futilely brushing at the streaks of mud clinging to her own habit. "I'd say *you've* had enough too, Meg."

She shot him an irritated glance as she righted her hat, which was listing drunkenly to one side. "I'm fine, Gervase!"

"Your habit is drenched. If you'd any sense—"

"A few splashes, nothing more! And I'm sure it will dry, once the sun comes out."

Lord Gervase glanced up at the overcast sky and raised an eloquent eyebrow, which Lady Margaret pointedly ignored as she turned back to her horse.

"Now, do stop fussing, and give me a leg up, Ger," she ordered.

For a moment, Hugo thought Lord Gervase would refuse outright; he certainly looked as though he wanted to. Then, mouth tightening, he held out his interlocked hands and boosted Lady Margaret into the saddle.

She thanked him punctiliously as she gathered up the reins and her dignity, biting her lip as she peered in the direction the leaders had gone. No need to point out the obvious, Hugo thought—that she'd have quite a ride to overtake the rest of the hunt. A ride made even more challenging because of her mount, a sturdy cob built for endurance rather than speed.

Lord Gervase crossed his arms. "Your kingdom for a horse?" he inquired, a decided edge to his voice.

Lady Margaret flushed, but her pretty face remained obstinate. "I *can* keep up, you aggravating boy—just see if I don't!" Head high, she touched her heel to the cob's side and urged it into a trot.

Lord Gervase stared after her, his eyes narrowed and his face set like stone.

"Ger," his sister began.

He held up a hand. "Say no more, Madeline. *I can see a church by daylight.*"

With that cryptic utterance, he remounted and set his own horse after Lady Margaret's.

Lady Madeline exhaled in obvious relief. "Good! She shouldn't come to harm, as long as he's got an eye on her."

"Is it my imagination, or does Lady Margaret think she has something to prove?" Hugo ventured, after a moment.

"She does—if only to herself. Namely, that she can keep up with Hal on the hunting field, or any of the pastimes he loves." Lady Madeline paused, then added, "They're engaged, you see—all but, anyway. The announcement's to be made at the ball, on the last night of the house party."

Hugo just managed to conceal his surprise. "But Lady Margaret's still in the schoolroom, isn't she?"

"Wellll... she's turned seventeen. It won't be long until she's out. And it *is* a very suitable match."

Hugo could not disagree with that. What could be more suitable than a duke's eldest son marrying another duke's eldest daughter? Denforth must be a good six or seven years older than his intended, but that wasn't an insurmountable gap. But the two seemed so different in temperament, as well as lacking the common interests that might bridge such a gap.

Apropos of which... Hugo couldn't help glancing in the direction Wilf and Miss Christabel had taken—together. Perhaps the cure to Lord Denforth's fascination for his brother lay in something that neither he nor Charley could have predicted: dimples, a pair of pansy-brown eyes, and a dauntless spirit on the field!

"Lord Saxby?" Lady Madeline's voice, sounding almost tentative, broke into his thoughts. "May I beg your assistance for a moment?"

"Ah. Of course."

She placed her boot in his interlaced hands and he lifted her up to the saddle, where she settled herself with the ease of an accomplished horsewoman. "Thank you, my lord. I'll be on my way now. Lysander," she nodded at the gelding, "is one of our strongest hunters. I'm sure you can catch up with the others if you gallop."

"Very likely, but I mean to accompany *you*." The declaration surprised him as much as it did her.

"There's no need for that!" Lady Madeline protested.

"I've ridden over these fields more times than I can count."

"Then I'll rely on you to guide us, but I insist on seeing you safely back to Denforth Castle, nonetheless." Hugo remounted the bay, took up the reins. "Now, let us be off, before you catch a chill in that wet habit."

She opened her mouth, closed it, then nodded, looking young and a little uncertain. "Very well, Lord Saxby. Thank you again."

They found a much narrower portion of the stream and crossed it without mishap, then started back the way they had come. Lady Madeline set a leisurely pace— giving the mare a chance to recover, Hugo realized and liked her the better for it. She might not care for sport as much as he did, but she knew how to treat her cattle.

She glanced at him through the veil of her riding-hat. "I can't say *I* much regret missing the hunt, but I am sorry to have taken you away from it, Lord Saxby."

"Not at all." And much to his surprise, Hugo found he meant it. After all, what was one hunt, when he'd ridden in so many?

My Dear Charley: Never before have I left a hunt before the kill...

No doubt she'd laugh herself into stitches at that one! And then avidly demand to know the reason why.

"It's kind of you to say so, Lord Saxby," the reason why observed. "And chivalrous of to offer your escort. Not many men would be so willing to forego a day's sport for such a reason. You ride splendidly, by the way —just as well as my brothers."

"Thank you. Having seen your brothers in the field, I realize this is no mean compliment. Lord Reginald, especially, rides like one born on horseback."

"Oh, Reg is practically a centaur!" she exclaimed, smiling. "He means to join a cavalry regiment once he's finished at university."

"He appears well-suited to it. *I* once dreamed of joining the army, but an heir's place is at home—or so I was told." *Especially after one's father suffers a crippling accident.* "So now I chase foxes instead of 'foes of England,'" Hugo added with a self-deprecating shrug.

She made a sympathetic moue. "Being the eldest isn't

always an unmitigated blessing, is it? Everyone expects *you* to be the responsible one."

"Ah. I'd forgot you and Denforth were twins. You were born first?"

"Ten minutes earlier, though sometimes it feels like ten years," she added, with a rueful little grimace. "And after today, it will almost certainly feel like *twenty*! My own fault—I always forget how punishing the pace can be in a hunt!"

"I gather you're not exactly an enthusiast, Lady Madeline?"

She flashed him a half-guilty smile. "Oh, I enjoy a good ride in the country, but I confess it's a matter of indifference to me whether or not we take a fox. Half the time, I'm quite happy to see it live to run another day. Heresy, I know!"

"The veriest blasphemy," Hugo agreed, grinning. "But your secret is safe with me, I assure you. So, what are your *preferred* activities?"

"Reading, dancing, and I have—well, something of a passion for the theatre."

"Seeing the latest plays, you mean?"

"Oh, certainly, but not *just* that. Putting on plays as well. Amateur theatricals," she explained. "And quite decent ones, if I do say so myself, with family and friends taking part. I suspect most people have a bit of frustrated actor in them. Denforth Castle has a salon that was made over into a private theatre years ago. So I couldn't possibly let it go to waste, *and* we've acquired some decent scenery and a wardrobe full of costumes too!"

"What plays do you put on?" Hugo asked, intrigued. He liked the theater well enough, but to judge from the light in her eyes, Lady Madeline was indeed *passionate* about it.

"Shakespeare, mostly, though we've also done a few French comedies to please *Maman*. We did *A Midsummer Night's Dream* last Whitsun." Lady Madeline smiled at the memory, her changeable eyes warming and her full lips curving; Hugo felt his heart give a curious stutter in his chest. "Our party was smaller than it is now, but we contrived nicely in spite of it all.

"I persuaded Gervase, Alasdair, Margaret, and Elaine

to be the four Athenians—they were the perfect age for it, and they play well against each other, though Ger balked at first, because he thought the lovers were too silly. He was very conscious of his dignity." Her lips quirked. "He still is, though perhaps a bit less stiff-necked about it now."

"Was Miss Christabel your Titania, by any chance?"

She shook her head. "Christabel is lovely to look at and she moves beautifully, but she has a memory like a sieve when it comes to recitation. She can't be trusted with any speech longer than a few lines, and sometimes not even then. I cast her as Peaseblossom, who has only to say 'Ready.' And for far too many rehearsals, she *wasn't*."

Hugo stifled a laugh. Lady Madeline's tongue was as sharp as her wit—and yet there was no malice in her assessment of her friend's abilities, or lack thereof. She was candid, even incisive, but not unkind. "How did you manage?"

"Her sister Olivia—our Hippolyta—took her in hand, fortunately and she had her lines down for the performance. *I* ended up playing Titania to Hal's Oberon, and Reg was Theseus."

Lady Madeline as the fairy queen. Hugo suspected she'd been enchanting in the part: elegant and regal, but with a touch of vulnerability; Titania did have her gentler moments. "And your Puck? That can be a hard role to play."

Her eyes took on a reminiscent gleam. "Oh, we'd a stroke of luck there! The Middleton boys brought along a friend of a friend—a Rufus Godolphin. He was *very* good—playing the part seemed to come naturally to him. I'm rather sorry he didn't come to *this* house party, but he's apparently a hard man to pin down. Pity."

"I take it you mean to stage a play this time too?" Hugo inquired.

She nodded. "Scenes from *Romeo and Juliet*—partly to help Juliana. Her governess, Miss Withersedge, is teaching it to her now, and she's finding it sadly dull. But seeing *Romeo and Juliet* put on, and taking part might change Juliana's mind. I do wish Mr. Joliffe hadn't retired," she added wistfully. "He was our tutor until two years ago—and he was *wonderful* when it came to plays and poetry."

"Lady Juliana seems a little young to play the lead."

"Oh, I have Elaine or Margaret in mind for that, but Juliana could still be a page or a lady in waiting. Same with Jason and the other children—we always try to include them in some way. Christabel can be Rosaline, so she won't have to memorize anything. And Hal wants to play Mercutio—*he* claims it's the only decent male role."

"It's certainly among the liveliest. Do you mean to have Lord Reginald as Tybalt?"

"Serve them both right if I did!" their sister retorted. "I've noticed that *Romeo and Juliet* seems quite popular with young men—mainly because of all the duels!"

Hugo chuckled. "Nothing like swordplay or murder to arouse interest, even among amateurs! I remember when I was at school, the most popular choices for acting out were Caesar's assassination and the fencing match between Hamlet and Laertes!"

"Did you get to play a part in either of them?"

"Yes, actually. I was a senator in *Julius Caesar*. And Fortinbras in *Hamlet*, coming in to clean up the mess afterwards."

Lady Madeline pulled a face. "Not the most rewarding of roles!"

"He's still alive at the end. *And* the King of Denmark as well as Norway."

"True," she conceded, lips twitching into a reluctant smile. "And it's a better fate than Rosencrantz and Guildenstern received." She paused and Hugo could sense what was coming next, even before she spoke again. "So—might I persuade you to lend *your* talents to this enterprise, Lord Saxby?"

Hugo opened his mouth to decline, politely, but what came out was not at all what he'd intended. "I'd—be happy to oblige, Lady Madeline, but I should warn you, I am the rankest of amateurs! You may end up putting me in a corner with no lines and a spear in my hand!"

"I very much doubt that, my lord!" Her eyes sparkled at him—bright, clear green at this moment, the exact shade of new leaves. "If you like, I can offer you first pick of *all* the men's roles, including Romeo!"

"Thank you, but that won't be necessary!" Hugo said

hastily. "It wouldn't be fair to have such an advantage over the rest of the cast, especially those with more stage experience than I. Besides, I think a... *mature* character might suit me better."

"Escalus, then," she suggested. "Or even Paris. We don't know his age, except that he's older than Juliet. But whoever you choose, I promise you won't regret taking part!"

Her enthusiasm was nothing if not infectious. Smiling back at her, a touch uncertainly, Hugo could only hope that she was right.

Chapter Four

All the world's a stage,
And all the men and women merely players...
—WILLIAM SHAKESPEARE, *As You Like It,*
   II, vii

MY DEAR CHARLEY: Never before have I taken part in an amateur theatrical.

Hugo mentally composed his letter, imagining his sister's eyes widening and brows arching in surprise. Well, it was true, wasn't it? Granted, not every house party he attended had the inclination or the materials to mount plays, but he'd always found elsewhere to be and other things to occupy him when such pastimes were proposed. At most, he'd participate in a game of Charades. Odd, perhaps, when he had rather liked pretending to be something or someone else during his and Charley's childhood games. Granted, as Robin Hood, he'd been free to make up his own dialogue, rather than memorize a speech—much less one in verse.

Yet here he was, in the midst of his first substantial scene in *Romeo and Juliet*—as Lord Capulet, opposite Lord Rupert Bonham who was playing Paris.

"But woo her, gentle Paris, get her heart / My will to her consent is but a part..."

Much to Hugo's surprise, the lines flowed smoothly from his tongue. The rhythm of speaking verse—drilled into him by various long-suffering tutors—had come back to him with remarkable speed over several days of rehearsal; he hadn't stumbled nearly as often as he'd expected. Lady Madeline had favored him with a nod of approval at the most recent read-through, which had made him feel absurdly pleased with himself.

What pleased him considerably less was having to work with Lord Rupert.

Never before have I been jealous of a younger man. Which was an utterly mortifying sensation that he wasn't about to impart to Charley or anyone else if he could avoid it.

Lord Rupert was handsome, there was no denying that, with curling dark hair and a warm olive complexion supposedly due to Spanish blood in the family. No doubt he'd look splendid in doublet and hose, once the costumes were distributed. And it wasn't as if he were incapable of speaking the verse, either. On the contrary: Bonham's delivery was smooth and his pronunciation impeccable, even if his performance tended to the superficial.

Hard not to feel positively middle-aged when acting opposite him, even though he was only two years younger than Hugo. He'd assured Lady Madeline he'd be most comfortable playing an older character. Now, perversely, he wished he'd put in a bid for one of the younger men's roles, after all. His only consolation was that she was playing *Lady Capulet*, which meant that they shared several scenes. Only fitting, as she'd got him into this—he still wasn't sure how.

But "the play was the thing," and Hugo's ambivalent feelings towards Bonham could not be allowed to interfere with his performance as Lord Capulet. Smiling genially at "Paris," he continued his speech:

> *"This night I hold an old accustomed feast*
> *Whereto I have invited many a guest,*
> *Such as I love; and you among the store,*
> *One more, most welcome, makes my number*
>   *more."*

"Well-done," Lady Madeline approved, when the scene was finished. "Though you need to project a bit more clearly on those last lines, Lord Saxby. And Lord

Rupert, could you show more of a reaction to what Lord Capulet is saying? You do want to marry his daughter, after all."

Bonham took the suggestion in good part, Hugo observed. Indeed, he'd noticed that the whole cast appeared to respect Lady Madeline's authority when it came to the play, showing no reluctance to take direction from a woman. But then, by her own account, she'd been in charge of these theatricals for years; no doubt everyone was accustomed to how she ran things.

As a newcomer, Hugo was fascinated, impressed, and just a little intimidated by her efficiency: her deft handling of so many different personalities, her detailed knowledge of stagecraft, and the seamless way she shifted between acting and directing.

Which she did now, taking the stage with Lady Elaine and Lady Margaret: the Capulet women meeting to discuss Juliet's possible marriage to Paris. Hugo positioned himself unobtrusively in the wings to watch. All three women were quite good, he realized after the first few lines: speaking the verse as though it came naturally, and obviously comfortable with each other. Lady Elaine was playing Juliet, but far from seeming disappointed about it, Lady Margaret had embraced the comic role of the Nurse, infusing the character's dialogue with a faint Yorkshire brogue that worked surprisingly well.

And then there was Lady Madeline, imbuing Lady Capulet with a simmering discontent that Hugo had never imagined when he thought about the character: a restlessness that suggested a woman not wholly comfortable with being a mother, nor, he realized with sudden clarity, entirely content as a wife to a man who must be many years her senior. Did he detect a note of wistfulness—even envy—in her voice when she remarked of Paris, "*Verona's summer hath not such a flower*"?

Denforth and his circle were also loitering in the wings, talking in low voices among themselves. Every now and then a phrase reached Hugo's ear, but he was too intent on Lady Madeline's performance to pay them much heed.

"—just *think* of the look on her face if I did," Denforth finished with a chuckle.

"You wouldn't dare." Lord Reginald spoke with a boredom approaching insolence.

Hugo winced inwardly, transferring his gaze from the scene onstage to the one backstage. He'd no idea what Denforth had proposed, but that was a red flag to a bull if he'd ever heard one. Once again, he wondered why the Lyons brothers always seemed to be at each other's throats.

"Oh, wouldn't I?" Denforth breathed, the light of battle in his eyes.

His brother smiled—no, smirked—unpleasantly. "I'd lay a guinea on it."

"Done."

Hell and damnation. No power on earth could halt a wager once money was involved. To which "her" could Denforth be referring? Hugo wondered, his unease growing. Lady Margaret, perhaps? Did the earl mean to play a prank on his future bride, and should she be warned if that was the case? Most likely he meant no harm, but the girl was so young and so very eager to please the man she was going to marry. He thought of Lady Margaret's face, pinched with fatigue but so determined as she urged her cob after the rest of the hunters, trying to prove she was up to her intended's speed. To make sport of her would be unkind—and unworthy of Denforth, for all his frivolity.

Hugo glanced back towards the stage, where Lady Capulet, Juliet, and the Nurse were finishing their conversation. He dared to breathe a little more easily when Lady Juliana entered as a servant to announce the arrival of the guests, and all four exited together, without incident.

But his misgivings revived when Denforth, sporting a particularly angelic expression, took his place onstage for the maskers' scene: a Mercutio ripe for any spree.

Things began well enough. Wilf was doing a decent job as Benvolio, the supportive friend and kinsman that Romeo—played by young Castlebrooke (Alasdair to his intimates)—needed. Hugo would be sure to compliment his brother later. Denforth was also behaving himself for the moment—until his first big speech. Sweeping to the front of the stage, the earl struck a pose and declaimed as he gesticulated extravagantly, "*O, then-a I see-a Queen-a*

Mab, she hath-a been with you-a! / She izza the fairies'-a mid-a-wife, and-a she comes—"

"Stop right there!" Lady Madeline's voice rang out, sharp as a newly whetted knife.

Hugo had to give Denforth credit: he didn't so much as flinch when his sister stalked towards him like an affronted cat.

"What was *that*?" she demanded, eyes narrowing as she stared down her twin.

"Mercutio, he is *italiano*!" Denforth insisted, flourishing his hands as a few other cast members tittered behind him.

Madeline closed her eyes for a moment, and spoke with strained patience. "He may be, but *you* are not."

"Oh, don't be such a stick-in-the-mud, Maddie!" her brother laughed. "The Nurse isn't from Yorkshire, but you like *Margaret's* accent well enough."

Out of the corner of his eye, Hugo saw Lady Margaret bite her lip and look down, clearly unsure whether to be pleased that Denforth had noticed her or embarrassed that he was using her to twit his sister.

"That's because what Margaret was doing actually worked *for* the part, not against it! Better not to attempt a foreign accent than to do it badly—especially as badly as that. *And* when it detracts from the play as a whole." Lady Madeline's gaze swept over them all with a searing intensity before she turned back to her brother. "We may be amateurs, but we are not *clowns*, and *Romeo and Juliet* is not meant to be a farce! Let's have that speech again—unaccented—from the opening line."

Denforth's eyes, still brimming with untrustworthy merriment, gazed into hers a moment longer. Then he shrugged and looked away, though Hugo saw him smirk in Lord Reginald's direction before resuming his lines. *"O, then I see Queen Mab hath been with you..."*

Hugo exhaled, taken aback to discover he'd barely breathed during that tense exchange.

"That was a close one." Lord Gervase had come up behind him, so quietly that Hugo hadn't heard him approach. "I'd credited Hal with more sense. Not that he has much at the best of times, but he knows how Madeline gets when she's directing a play."

"Lord Reginald may have put him up to it."

"Ah. That explains a good deal." Lord Gervase's eyes flickered towards his elder sister. "She's a slave driver, you know—and not merely over amateur theatricals. But she works as hard as anyone else—harder, really—to make something worthwhile happen, so we forgive her."

Hugo followed the direction of his gaze. "And respect her?"

"That, too. Even Hal, though he'd be boiled in oil before he admitted as much." Lord Gervase paused, then added lightly, "*I tell you, he that can lay hold of her / Shall have the chinks.* And a good deal more besides."

Startled, Hugo turned to stare at him, but Lord Gervase was already drifting off towards another section of the wings, where Lady Elaine and Lady Margaret were sitting.

She works hard, to make something worthwhile happen.

Handsome praise, coming as it did from a brother, Hugo thought as he glanced towards the stage again. Denforth had stopped playing the fool and was now delivering a creditable rendition of the Queen Mab speech beneath Lady Madeline's watchful eye.

Visions of her unfolded in Hugo's imagination: running a household, raising a family, presiding over countless social functions, all with the same focus and intensity she brought to this. The same *passion* to make something as good—as worthwhile—as it could possibly be.

A duke's daughter. An unconventional beauty whose presence drew him like a lodestone. A woman of wit, will, and steely determination. *And a good deal more besides.*

※

UNDER THE CIRCUMSTANCES, Madeline thought it best to propose a break for tea after the maskers' scene. Hal had sailed through the rest of the Queen Mab speech, looking all the while as though butter wouldn't melt in his mouth. And Alasdair-as-Romeo had ended the scene on a note of foreboding, as though he sensed the doom that was to come, even as he accepted his fate.

Madeline had praised his interpretation, commended the other players (Hal included), and generally did her best to pretend that her twin's earlier prank had never taken place. As it was, she strongly suspected who'd put him up to it, and it wouldn't do to encourage either of them.

Tea had been laid out in an adjoining room, and the cast promptly descended upon the refreshments as though they hadn't seen food for a week. After which they separated into small groups, laughing and talking among themselves. Much to her satisfaction, Madeline saw Alasdair and Elaine sharing a corner: acting opposite each other seemed to have brought them closer together. They might not know it yet, but the course of true love appeared to be running quite smoothly for them.

Finding a quiet corner of her own, Madeline sipped her tea, appreciating the way the hot liquid soothed her throat, nibbled at sandwiches and ginger cakes—and allowed herself to relax for the first time in hours. The play *was* shaping well, and the performers all seemed to be tackling their roles with enthusiasm and good cheer. The rain that had dampened outdoor pursuits for the last three days might have had something to do with that: even the most avid sportsman might prefer a warm theater to a sodden covert in the middle of a downpour.

Apropos of which... searching the room, she spied Lord Saxby by the sideboard, pouring himself a cup of tea. Setting her cup aside, she unashamedly admired the view. The gas lamps shone on Saxby's fair hair like a halo, though his face and form were delightfully of *this* world.

Such an attractive man—and as agreeable to speak with as he was to look at. No point in denying that, of all the potential suitors attending this house party, she liked him best. Lord Rupert was a handsome flirt, while the Honorable Clarence Moresby seemed more interested in sport than anything else. Lord Saxby was also an enthusiastic sportsman, but judging from his chivalry on the day of the hunt, other things mattered to him as well.

And he seemed to have taken to acting with a good grace, though she was surprised that he'd chosen Lord Capulet, of all parts! But he'd been firm about his choice, so she'd given up on further attempts to persuade him otherwise. At least they shared some scenes: Lady Capulet's feelings for her husband might not be of the warmest—Madeline thought she showed more affection for her nephew, Tybalt—but that did not change the fact that they were Juliet's parents.

Picking up her empty plate, she left her corner and joined him at the sideboard. A hostess should see to the comfort of her guest, after all.

"Is everything to your liking, Lord Saxby?" she inquired. "I hope you'll try the ginger cakes. They're a particular specialty of Mrs. Hill's, especially during the Christmas season."

He glanced up, smiling. "Thank you—they smell very appetizing." He placed two cakes on his plate. "Anything else you'd recommend?"

"The deviled ham sandwiches are always good, if you like spices." Madeline selected one, along with another ginger cake.

"Very warming, on a cold day." Lord Saxby took two sandwiches and a sausage roll, then glanced around the room, clearly looking for a place to sit.

"You can share my alcove, if you like," Madeline offered, trying to sound casual. "It's quiet and it overlooks the Italian Garden, even if all you can see right now is rain."

He paused, then smiled. "Thank you, Lady Madeline. That would be pleasant."

Fortunately, the window seat was long enough for two—just. Despite the six inches or so between them, maintained for propriety's sake, Madeline could feel the warmth from Lord Saxby's body and breathe in the scent of his cologne: something pleasantly sharp and lemony. Outside, the rain continued to fall, pattering softly to the ground and streaking the windowpane with silvery runnels like tears.

Finishing her cake, Madeline set her empty plate on the broad sill behind them. "Just a little over a week to Christmas," she mused aloud. "Where does the time go?"

"Christmas always seems to approach at a gallop," Saxby agreed. "Not that *I* mind! I heard one of the maids singing 'The Holly and the Ivy' this morning as she went about her business, and I was dashed tempted to join in."

"You'll hear a lot more of that in days to come,"

Madeline informed him. "We always have Christmas music here. Elaine and Juliana are forever singing one carol or other once the greenery's brought in, or the snow starts to fall."

"White Christmases must be the general rule this far north."

"More often than not. It would be nice to have snow, instead of all this rain. Even if it *has* made people more amenable to staying indoors and learning their lines!"

"Given the season, I'm a little surprised that you're not doing a Nativity play, instead of *Romeo and Juliet*," he remarked.

"We did a Nativity play once when I was sixteen," she confessed, "but were expressly forbidden by our parents ever to attempt another."

His brows shot up. "Good Lord, as bad as that?"

"We had the brilliant idea to stage it in a tithe-barn, with live animals." Madeline shuddered at the memory. "Never again! Hal swore up and down that Mary's donkey wouldn't disgrace itself at a pivotal moment, but..." She pulled a face. "You can imagine the rest!"

Lord Saxby chuckled. "Blame it on the natural contrariness of donkeys!"

Her lips twitched in an answering smile. "Capulets and Montagues are child's play by comparison! Speaking of which, are you enjoying rehearsals? I thought you did very well today."

"Thank you. As it happens, I *am* enjoying being in the play, more than I thought I would." He paused, his brown eyes serious. "You and your family have set a high standard, especially when it comes to speaking the verse. I don't want to let you down."

The commendation surprised and touched her. "You haven't so far, Lord Saxby. I think even our Mr. Joliffe would approve of your delivery. And he would never tolerate sloppy elocution from his students!"

He brightened visibly. "You relieve me, Lady Madeline. Perhaps I shan't embarrass myself, after all."

"We have two more days of rehearsal," she reminded him. "And a costume fitting tomorrow. Costumes always help. It's so much easier to believe you're who you're pretending to be—king, prince, beggar—when you look the part. We always have at least one dress rehearsal before the actual performance." And Madeline would ensure that Lord Capulet was handsomely garbed, as befitted the character's station—and his portrayer's manly attributes.

The men playing the younger roles would have first claim on doublet and hose, she reflected. But there were rich-looking robes and tunics suitable for older roles: and who was to say that Juliet's father wasn't still a fine figure of a man? Something in dark blue or deep red, to emphasize Lord Saxby's fair coloring and make it shine like a crown...

"Lady Madeline?" Her name, spoken in Saxby's rich baritone, recalled her to the present.

"Forgive me, Lord Saxby." She gave him her most winning smile, surprised at how natural it felt to smile at *him*. "My mind wandered for a moment.'

"Understandable, given how much you have to occupy it. I just wanted to tell you how impressed I've been by your Lady Capulet. I'd never thought much about the character before," he added. "But your interpretation has made me want to take a closer look at her."

"Thank you for the compliment, my lord. I've found that if you go back to a play and look it over carefully, you can find things that tell you more about a character, which can help shape your performance," she explained. "Even casual utterances like Lady Capulet mentioning that she was close to Juliet's age when she became a mother. Whereas Lord Capulet—"

"Must be forty, if he's a day," he finished.

"Closer to fifty, I'd say. Remember when he and his cousin are reminiscing about going masking thirty years earlier?"

Lord Saxby winced. "Ah, yes. I'd almost forgotten."

Madeline raised inquiring brows. "Regretting your choice? I still think you'd have made a splendid Prince Escalus."

"I'm afraid I've always considered Escalus a rather thankless role," he confessed. "He's the fellow who shows up now and then to scold everyone, but to whom no one *listens* until it's too late. Not even his cousin Mercutio heeds him, which doesn't say much about his influence—or his effectiveness as a ruler!"

She hid a smile. "There's something to that, I'll concede."

"At least Lord Capulet has a part in the main action," he went on, warming to his theme. "And I have the added compensation of sharing scenes with *you*."

Madeline stilled. So did Lord Saxby, as though just realizing what he'd said. They stared at each other, the silence between them so pronounced that it was like a sound in itself.

Madeline could *feel* her face heating. *Now comes the wanton blood up in your cheeks: / They'll be in scarlet straight at any news.* A swarm of butterflies seemed to have taken wing in her stomach as well, their flutterings intensifying with every moment that she gazed into Lord Saxby's warm brown eyes. But an answering warmth was also spreading through her, golden as honey and every bit as sweet.

Was this what it felt like—to fall in love?

"Maddie!"

And suddenly Juliana was there, bright-eyed, eager, and completely oblivious to the undercurrents between her elders. "Are we going back to the theater soon?" she asked, glancing from her sister to Lord Saxby. "We've got three more acts to get through."

Madeline cleared her throat and rose from the window seat, avoiding Lord Saxby's eyes. "Of course, darling. Let's round everyone up now, shall we?"

❄

THREE NIGHTS LATER, Hugo peered out from the wings into the rapidly filling auditorium, the sea of expectant faces, and swallowed hard. Withdrawing into the shadows, he let the curtain drop into place, tried to calm his pounding heart. If *this* was stage fright, then he had the deepest sympathy for every player who'd ever trod the boards!

A rustle of satin behind him, accompanied by the beguiling fragrance of rose and neroli. "Nervous, my lord husband?"

Hugo exhaled, turned to face Lady Madeline, regal in wine brocade trimmed with sable, her dark hair confined within a jeweled net. Costumes did indeed make a difference: she looked like a Renaissance portrait come to life. "Petrified. My one consolation is that no one will see my knees knocking together under *this*." He indicated Lord Capulet's heavy velvet robe, which fell nearly to his ankles.

She reached out, touched his sleeve gently. "You'll be fine! You were flawless at our last rehearsal—unlike some I could mention."

Despite his apprehension, Hugo felt his mouth twitch in a reluctant smile. The final dress rehearsal had been nothing if not memorable. Some half a dozen cast members had forgotten lines they'd known perfectly the day before; Castlebrooke had almost poked Lord Reginald in the eye with his foil, for which he'd apologized profusely; and Lord Reginald had knocked Denforth on his backside during the Tybalt-Mercutio duel, for which he'd apologized not at all. Somehow, Lady Madeline had kept the ship afloat, saying with tight-lipped tolerance that it was best that they got all the mistakes out of the way beforehand. "I can only hope that means the performance itself will be perfect."

"So do we all! But we have two prompters, just in case, and you can depend on me if you have trouble in our scenes. But I think it will be fine," she added bracingly. "And so will you."

Buoyed by her encouragement, he mustered a smile. "I shall endeavor not to disappoint."

After their conversation three days earlier, he'd gone looking for more interesting facets to explore in Lord Capulet. A doting father—who could become choleric and unreasonable when crossed. A husband unsure of his wife's affections. A man's man, out of his depth at dealing with women, by turns frustrated and confused by them, and apt to bluster when he felt most insecure.

He wasn't sure how much of the cast had paid attention to his interpretation, but he'd glimpsed a spark of approval in Lady Madeline's eyes during one of their more charged scenes together. At the very least he had the satisfaction of knowing that he was giving her Lady Capulet a more interesting foil to play opposite.

She smiled back at him now before turning to the rest of the cast, who'd gathered in the wings behind them. "Five minutes to curtain. Places, everyone!"

Those five minutes seemed to last an eternity—and then not long enough. Waiting in position with Lady Madeline, Hugo watched as the curtain rose upon a courtyard in Verona, where the feuding Capulets and Montagues stood with drawn swords and upraised fists, but frozen in place like figures in a tableau. An appreciative murmur arose from the audience, and Hugo felt Lady Madeline relax beside him. So, for all her poise, she was *not* immune to nerves, but then as director, the success of this play, of this *vision*, rested largely on her shoulders. He sent her a reassuring smile, as Lord Gervase as Chorus strolled onstage to deliver the prologue.

"Two households, both alike in dignity, / In fair Verona, where we lay our scene…"

He'd a fine speaking voice, Hugo thought as he listened. Perhaps even better than his brothers': clear and resonant, with a gravity that made him seem older than his years. A definite advantage, as Lord Gervase would be doubling as Friar Laurence later in the play.

The prologue ended, and the Chorus melted into the crowd, which immediately unfroze and began to brawl. Seconds later, Wilf-as-Benvolio ran onstage to part one set of combatants, only to be engaged by Lord Reginald's fiery Tybalt, forever bristling and spoiling for a fight. The part of Hugo that was not awaiting his cue experienced a pang of pride that his brother was giving a good performance as the earnest, peace-loving young Montague.

The cue came at last, and Hugo hurried onstage, scowling mightily, with Lady Capulet at his heels. *"What noise is this?"* he bellowed. *"Give me my long sword, ho!"*

Lady Madeline's voice rang out in mocking response. *"A crutch, a crutch! Why call you for a sword?"*

Hugo spared "his wife" a withering glance, but continued to demand a weapon while glowering across the stage at Branscombe, whom Lady Madeline had persuaded—through some sorcery, no doubt—to take on the small role of Lord Montague. Getting into the spirit of things, Branscombe glared back and lunged towards him, restrained only by Olivia Middleton's Lady Montague pulling on his sleeve.

All around him, Hugo could sense the energy rising, along with the enthusiasm, as his fellow actors threw themselves into their parts, surpassing their earlier efforts in rehearsal. By the time the Capulets' feast began, it was clear that, if not perfect, this production was on its way to being very good indeed.

The star-crossed lovers dominated the first half of the play, so Hugo spent the scenes when he wasn't onstage watching from the wings. During rehearsals, he'd developed a strong appreciation for many of the younger cast members. Lady Elaine was appropriately innocent and sweet as Juliet, but there was a budding maturity to her portrayal as well: a sense of a girl becoming a woman almost overnight after falling in love. And Castlebrooke played up to her with a sincerity that some Romeos lacked. Hadn't Lady Madeline hinted at an attachment between them? It worked to good effect here, to have a Romeo genuinely attracted to his Juliet and hanging with rapt fascination on her every word during the balcony scene.

Meanwhile, Lord Gervase transformed effortlessly into Friar Laurence, donning a coarse brown habit and a greying tonsured wig while his bearing and speech patterns altered subtly to those of a much older man. And Lady Margaret, her slim figure padded with pillows under a loose gown, worked a similar magic as the earthy Nurse, whose Yorkshire brogue lent itself admirably to the bawdier speeches. And Denforth made a dashing, spirited Mercutio—Hugo suspected that the earl was essentially playing himself, but it was still a good performance, and the character's death moved several ladies in the audience to tears.

Once Mercutio and Tybalt were slain, the older generation came to the fore again. As Lord Capulet, Hugo watched aghast as his wife flung herself, alternately weeping and raging, on Tybalt's corpse. Madeline had dispensed with her coif, so her hair spilled wildly over her shoulders like a Maenad's, and her eyes burned with grief and fury as she demanded of Escalus, "*I beg for justice, which thou, Prince, must give. / Romeo slew Tybalt; Romeo must not live!*"

Then it was Lord Capulet's turn to rant and storm as his formerly docile daughter resisted his plan to marry her to Paris. Hugo did his best to convey confusion and disappointment as well as temper as Capulet railed at

Juliet, even dragging her from her bed and flinging her to the floor—Lady Elaine's suggestion, which hadn't stopped Castlebrooke from glaring daggers at Hugo the first time they'd tried it in rehearsal.

A few scenes later, standing over the seemingly dead Juliet, Hugo let his shoulders drop as though bowed by the weight of the world as he numbly pronounced his only child's epitaph: "*Death lies on her like an untimely frost / Upon the sweetest flower of the field.*" United in grief, Lord and Lady Capulet withdrew, leaning heavily on each other as they made their exit.

Once in the wings, Lady Madeline straightened up and smiled at Hugo. Despite the rigors of the scene they'd just played, her eyes were shining. "That was marvelous," she breathed, squeezing his forearm. "I think we've *done* the thing, my lord!"

Infected by her excitement, he grinned back at her. "I'd say we have, my lady! You were brilliant, by the way."

"So were you! Now, all that remains is for Alasdair and Elaine to bring it home. And they will," she predicted with complete confidence.

Lady Madeline's faith in her two leads proved more than justified. Watching from the wings once more, Hugo felt his eyes sting and his throat tighten as Friar Laurence's plan to reunite the lovers went horribly, tragically awry; as a grieving, defiant Romeo drank poison to join his wife in heaven; as Juliet unhesitatingly stabbed herself and fell lifeless across her husband's body, their limp hands meeting in one last "holy palmer's kiss." Beside him, Lady Madeline stood like a statue, her lips parted and her own eyes suspiciously bright.

Moments later, they were back onstage for the final scene, as Capulets and Montagues learned the full extent of the lovers' tragedy. Hugo did not have to feign the emotion that hoarsened his voice as Lord Capulet extended his hand to his old enemy and offered the peace that had come too late to save their children. And as Escalus somberly uttered the last lines, the feuding families now moved to embrace, freezing into position once again as the curtain fell.

A moment of silence yielded to thunderous applause and even an enthusiastic whistle or two. Taking his bows with the rest of the cast, Hugo felt a heady rush of accomplishment and exhilaration unlike anything he'd experienced before. While he wasn't sure he wanted to make a habit of appearing in amateur theatricals, by God, he could finally understand their appeal!

Especially when acting opposite someone like Lady Madeline. Catching her eye, he sent her a tentative smile, to which she returned an incandescent one, fit to launch a thousand ships.

Never before have I felt so alive.

THE DOUBLETS AND HOSE, the coifs and wimples, the farthingales and stomachers had all been put away, the swords and bucklers returned to the prop boxes. And everyone who'd been a part of tonight's performance had been acknowledged and thanked, from the cast to the small cadre of servants who'd kept things running smoothly behind the scenes.

"*Our revels now are ended,*" Madeline murmured as she fastened a locket on a fine gold chain about her throat and shook out the skirts of her rose-red evening gown, bright as her mood.

Tomorrow, everyday life would resume, and she suspected there would be a number of aching heads in the morning, along with a general sense of anticlimax. But tonight was for celebration. As had become the tradition after their amateur theatricals, an elaborate buffet supper awaited them all in the Grand Salon, courtesy of *Maman*.

Accepting a gold tissue shawl from Albertine, Madeline draped it over her shoulders and hurried downstairs to join her castmates. One castmate in particular, she acknowledged with a secret smile. She only hoped that Lord Saxby wouldn't be too hard to find in the crowd— or excessively besieged by new female admirers!

As expected, the Grand Salon was teeming with people, several of whom descended upon Madeline the moment they saw her, lavishly praising the play and her performance.

"*Trés bien, chérie!*" her mother pronounced, kissing her

lightly on both cheeks. "You and the others have out-done yourselves tonight!"

Smiling, Madeline thanked her and returned the salute, before accepting the equally heartfelt congratulations of the Duchess of Langdale and Lady Middleton. Fortunately, Elaine and Margaret entered the salon a few minutes later, freeing her to go in search of Lord Saxby.

Spying him in a group of several young men that included two of her brothers, she made her way towards them.

"We always have a good turn-out for our shooting parties," Hal was saying as she approached. "Mind you, the weather can make a big difference to one's success in the field!"

"Not necessarily," Reg pointed out with typical contrariness, and Madeline stifled a sigh. "A *superior* marksman can bring down a bird in any conditions."

The implication was as obvious as it was insulting, and Hal flushed, his blue eyes narrowing. "Shall we make a wager, then, *Reggie?*" he inquired, using the diminutive their brother hated most. "Five guineas says I bag more birds than you on New Year's Day."

"Keep your money, Little Harold." Reg's voice was deceptively soft. "I promise to eat all of *your* killing."

"Wrong play," Madeline interposed crisply, stepping between them. Much as she longed to crack her brothers' heads together, a conciliatory approach was more likely to work, so she favored them with her sweetest smile. "Can we not concentrate on *tonight,* instead? I wanted to tell you how splendid you were in the play. *All* of you," she added, noticing that Lord Rupert Bonham and Mr. Moresby were also in the group. "It was a pleasure to perform with you."

They preened at that, even Hal and Reg, and Lord Saxby sketched her a bow. "Thank you, Madam Director. I believe I speak for us all when I say you brought out the best in us."

Murmurs of "hear, hear" and "quite so" greeted his remark. Touched, Madeline thanked them, then turned to her twin.

"By the by, Hal, Margaret's come down," she informed him brightly. "I'm sure she'd be delighted if you brought her some refreshment. You know she's one of those who can't eat a morsel before going onstage!"

Their eyes locked, and Madeline could almost *see* the wheels turning in her twin's head as he weighed the merits of staying to bandy words with Reg or waiting upon a betrothed he regarded as another sister. The latter won out, barely; Hal turned away with a shrug and a slightly martyred air. "Ah. If you'll excuse me, everyone —duty calls."

He strolled away and Madeline gritted her teeth, relieved that Margaret was in no position to have heard that graceless remark. But at least her friend would receive *some* attention from her soon-to-be-fiancé. Better still, Hal and Reg had been separated—for the moment.

"Talking of refreshments," Lord Saxby began, "may I escort you to the buffet table, Lady Madeline? You must be quite hungry yourself, by now."

"Famished, my lord, so I accept your invitation with pleasure. Gentlemen." She nodded to them as she passed, her hand resting on the crook of Saxby's arm.

"Deftly managed, finding a way to send Denforth off like that," he observed.

"There are advantages, sometimes, to being the eldest."

"Are Denforth and Lord Reginald always so... competitive?"

"I'm afraid so," she admitted. "I suspect it's often difficult, when the heir and the spare are close in age—and want so many of the same things! I can't remember a time when they weren't at odds." Which wasn't helped, she reflected, by Father favoring Hal and *Maman* Reg.

"And your other two brothers? Are they part of this rivalry as well?"

Madeline shook her head. "Jason's too young to be caught up in this. And Gervase tends to stay out of it, unless he sees some particular advantage to getting involved. Mostly, he goes his own way." She gave Lord Saxby a rueful smile. "I imagine things are a good deal more peaceful in your family."

"They're quieter, perhaps," he acknowledged. "But my sister Charley might argue about whether that's a good thing. *She* thinks my life needs stirring up!"

"Truly?" Smiling, Madeline tightened her hold on his

arm. "Well, in that respect, the Lyons family is more than happy to oblige!"

"It seems a task to which you and yours are eminently suited," Lord Saxby agreed, his eyes crinkling. "Ah, supper!" He gestured to the laden table before them. "Anything in particular tempt your appetite, my lady?"

"*All* of it does," she confessed, hungrily surveying the platters heaped high with French and English delicacies. "But I'm partial to just about anything with lobster! And Mrs. Hill makes these wonderful chicken and mushroom *vol-au-vents*, and *petit-fours*..."

"Say no more." Lord Saxby set about preparing plates for them both. He was just pouring out two glasses of champagne, when Madeline sensed a familiar presence behind them.

Her blood chilled even before he spoke, his rich baritone as warm and jovial as she remembered. "Madeline, my dear! I was hoping I might find you in this crush."

Schooling her features into a mask of perfect courtesy, she turned to face him. "Good evening, Father."

❄

WHAT THE DEVIL...?

Hugo stared at Lady Madeline who, with the utterance of three words, had seemingly changed from a warm, vibrant woman into a cool, remote effigy—Galatea reverting to a statue. Dismayed, he transferred his gaze to the man who had effected the transformation: the Duke of Whitborough himself.

"And Lord Saxby," His Grace continued, turning a genial smile on Hugo. "My compliments on your performance! I've seen *Romeo and Juliet* put on several times, but can't recall a more memorable Lord Capulet."

"Thank you, Duke," Hugo replied, a touch guardedly, his eyes still on Lady Madeline.

"And you, my dear," Whitborough set his hands on his daughter's shoulders, "surpassed yourself in every way."

"Thank you, Father." Lady Madeline stood perfectly still, let the duke embrace her and then kiss her brow, but her own arms remained at her sides.

Hugo's uneasiness grew. Perhaps playing Lord Capulet had honed his instincts, but just as Juliet had hidden her true feelings beneath a show of docility, he suspected that Lady Madeline was doing likewise. Impossible not to wonder what those feelings were: Love? Hate? Betrayal? Certainly not indifference.

If Whitborough noticed his daughter's constraint, he concealed it well. "You should be proud of your triumph tonight. I know *I* am." He released her, still smiling. "Enjoy your evening, sweetheart—and try not to drink too much champagne! You'll only regret it in the morning."

The corners of her mouth turned up briefly at that, then flattened again as Whitborough strode off through the crowd. Her changeable eyes were stormy green—and stark with misery.

Oh, my dear. The words rose involuntarily to Hugo's lips, he swallowed them at once, cleared his throat instead. "Lady Madeline—"

She closed her eyes for a moment, opened them with a determined smile. "Shall we find ourselves a corner, Lord Saxby—before the lobster puffs get cold and the champagne gets warm? There's absolutely nothing worse than warm champagne, you know!"

His heart ached at the forced gaiety in her voice, the gallant show she was putting on, but unless she chose to confide in him, he could only humor her. "An excellent idea. Shall we try one of the window alcoves?"

Plates and glasses in hand, they skirted the perimeter of the salon floor, finding a cozy window embrasure on the far side of the room where they could enjoy their feast. Food and drink revived Lady Madeline's spirits, and soon they were conversing easily, sharing their favorite moments of tonight's performance.

"A toast to you, my lady." Hugo raised his glass. "For proving me wrong! I never thought I'd enjoy acting as much as I did."

She raised her brows. "Enough to do it again, someday?"

"I don't know about *that*!" he amended hastily. "Let's just say—I wouldn't immediately refuse to take part, if asked."

"Fair enough." She smiled then, a radiant, unshadowed smile that stole his breath. "It *has* been a wonderful evening, hasn't it?"

"One of the best I've spent," Hugo agreed.

"You might feel a bit flat tomorrow," she warned. "*I* tend to, the day after—the low coming after the high. Fortunately, there's the ball to look forward to, along with Christmas."

"I imagine you celebrate it in lavish style, here at Denforth?"

"But, of course—our family never does things by halves!" Lady Madeline's eyes brightened as she warmed to her theme. "We put up a tree—the finest, tallest one that can be found—and we make a party of decorating it, no later than Christmas Eve. *Maman* even had special ornaments made for each one of us—marked with our initial—and we hang them ourselves. And we arrange the presents under the tree."

"You don't have the servants do that for you?"

"Why should they have all the fun? And there are carols and concerts. Father sometimes engages singers or actors for special performances here—professionals, unlike ourselves. And there's sport as well," she added. "Another hunt on St. Stephen's Day, and sometimes a shooting party in the New Year. And then there's a feast on Twelfth Night, where we crown the Lord of Misrule. We celebrate through the sixth of January, really."

Hugo shook his head as he thought of his own parents, wintering sedately in Somerset. "The Lowells have always celebrated Christmas quietly. Your family's stamina amazes me."

Her eyes danced. "We just happen to have a high capacity for enjoyment, although we try to be considerate of those who appreciate peace and quiet too. Talking of which," she paused, coloring slightly, "some of our current guests will be staying on for Christmas. I had wondered, Lord Saxby, if you would... be interested in doing so?"

She sounded almost tentative, unlike her usual, supremely confident self.

"I'm afraid that—I am already promised elsewhere for Christmas." Hugo could taste the regret in his refusal. "It would be discourteous to my hosts... to change my plans at the last minute." Much as he wanted to.

Dear God, how he wanted to—especially with Lady Madeline so near, bright and beautiful in a scarlet gown that lent a tinge of gold to her ivory skin.

Never before have I been more tempted to break my word...

She lowered her eyes. "I understand. Lord Saxby. No gentleman could do otherwise. But I hope you'll consider paying us a visit, perhaps sometime in the New Year?"

Hugo swallowed. "I would be happy to revisit Yorkshire—and Denforth." *And you.*

Lady Madeline glanced up, *that* smile hovering about her lips again. "You would be most welcome, my lord. Oh, look!" she exclaimed suddenly. "It's snowing!"

Following her gaze, Hugo saw that feathery white flakes had indeed begun to fall on the other side of the glass.

Lady Madeline's expression grew soft, even dreamy. "No matter how old I get, I never tire of the sight. I may feel differently in two months' time, but the first snow of the season..."

"There *is* something almost magical about it." *And* about this moment, Hugo thought.

They sat in companionable silence, watching the snow descend.

Chapter Five

*—*WILLIAM SHAKESPEARE, *A Midsummer*
Night's Dream, II, i

21 December 1879

WINTER SOLSTICE. THE SHORTEST DAY of the year, followed by the longest night. An appropriate occasion for
a ball—especially one that was to celebrate the betrothal
of Whitborough's heir, Hugo mused as he entered the
ballroom.

The surroundings were certainly festive enough:
hangings of green and gold silk warmed the salon's pale
walls, with hints of scarlet and white in the floral
arrangements: berried holly interspersed with
"Christmas roses" and pearly sprigs of mistletoe. Hugo
even spied several pots of velvety red poinsettias, most
likely grown in the Whitboroughs' conservatory.

A number of guests had already assembled, and to
Hugo's pleasure, Lady Madeline was among them. A
small part of him wondered how it was that he could
pick her out so readily in a crowd, but he disregarded it
as he made his way towards her.

Approaching, he saw that she was surrounded by the
youngest members of the house party: Lady Juliana,

Lord Jason, Lady Alicia Carlisle, and Miss Susannah Middleton.

"Margaret and Alicia are going to adopt one kitten and share her between them. The Middletons said they'll take one when it's old enough. And Alasdair said he might take *two*," Lady Juliana was telling her sister. "To keep the mice in check at his country estate."

"Very obliging of him," Lady Madeline remarked. "At this rate, my dressing room will soon be untenanted!"

"You're still keeping the kittens in your dressing room?" Hugo exclaimed, surprised.

The Lyons sisters both looked up, Lady Madeline flushing just a little. "Under the circumstances, it didn't seem quite right to evict them or Volumnia," she explained. "Not at Christmas. After the New Year, however," she leveled a stern gaze at her sister, "I expect you to find other accommodations for them, Ju!"

"I'll think of something," Lady Juliana promised. "Good evening, Lord Saxby," she added with her winsome smile.

"And to you, Lady Juliana. You're staying for the party?" Hugo inquired, eyeing her blue velvet frock and matching hair ribbon.

She nodded. "For the first hour or so—because of the Important Announcement."

"Lord Denforth and Meg are getting married!" Lady Alicia—twelve, blonde, and angelically pretty—clapped her hands together with excitement. "Isn't it romantic?"

"*Engaged*, Alicia," Lady Juliana corrected. "They aren't anywhere near ready to be married. Your sister's not even out yet."

"Well, I hope she makes me a bridesmaid," Lady Alicia sighed, ignoring these dampening words.

"*I* hope there'll be pudding," Lord Jason, a dark, quiet, slightly pudgy child, remarked "We didn't have any at dinner, before."

"I wonder if there will be trifle," eleven-year-old Susannah Middleton added wistfully. "Or jam tarts."

"I suspect there will be both,' Lady Madeline replied, smiling indulgently. "Just try not to overeat, all of you, or you'll feel wretched later."

Assuring her that they had no such intention, the children began to discuss among themselves their favorite holiday treats. Seizing his chance, Hugo offered Lady Madeline his arm. "Will you walk with me a moment, my lady?"

"Of course, Lord Saxby." Resting her hand on his elbow, she let him draw her away from her juniors.

"First of all," Hugo began, "I had to tell you how lovely you look tonight."

"Thank you." A trifle self-consciously, she toyed with the lace edging her bodice. "I seldom wear pink, but Margaret will be in green this evening, so I thought it best to choose another color. Something a bit... quieter than my usual style."

"Well, it suits you nonetheless." Her gown was a soft rose, embroidered with velvety petals in a deeper shade of pink. On anyone else it might have appeared a touch insipid; on Lady Madeline, it bewitched, making her look—not less formidable, but warmer and more approachable. Like a rose in winter.

As though reading his thoughts, Lady Madeline quoted, *"At Christmas, I no more desire a rose, / Than wish a snow in May's new-fangled mirth—"*

"But like of each thing that in season grows," Hugo finished triumphantly.

Her eyes widened. "You are full of surprises tonight, Lord Saxby!"

"My present company has taught me the virtue of surprises. I never realized just how much Shakespeare I'd absorbed until I came here." Hugo paused, smiling into Lady Madeline's sparkling green eyes. "And a beautiful woman is always in season, whatever color she wears."

"Flattery may get you somewhere, my lord," she said lightly, though he could tell that the compliment pleased her.

"Will it get me one of your waltzes tonight?" he asked.

She consulted her programme. "As it happens, my second waltz of the evening is yet unclaimed. As is the supper dance. In recompense for such a pretty speech— to say nothing of capping my quotation—I feel I must put you down for both, Lord Saxby!"

Hugo inclined his head "As my lady wishes."

The increasing hum of conversation around them attested to the arrival of more guests. The Whitboroughs had invited many local families as well, Lady Madeline explained: mutual friends of themselves and the Carlisles. The influx pressed Hugo into closer proximity to his companion, which he did not mind in the least. Lady Madeline still smelled delightfully of rose and neroli, with the faintest hint of spice that reminded him of clove-studded pomander balls.

Meanwhile, footmen had begun to circulate, bearing silver trays holding crystal flutes of champagne, which they offered to the guests. Hugo took two flutes when a footman paused before him, handing one to Lady Madeline.

"Our best vintage, of course." She held her glass up to the light as the tiny bubbles winked and popped in the wine. "*Maman* would have nothing less for such an occasion. Ah." Her hand tightened about the stem. "*Behold, the bridegroom draweth nigh...*"

Hugo followed her gaze to where both sets of ducal parents were descending a marble staircase into the ballroom. The newly engaged pair followed, Lady Margaret in a pale green gown, with delicate white flowers in her chestnut hair, looking almost heartrendingly young. And glowing with adoration for the golden young man beside her—whose expression was far less enraptured, Hugo noted with some trepidation. Indeed, of the six, only Denforth wasn't smiling. At best he appeared resigned, but his mouth had a slightly sulky set.

"For heaven's sake, Hal," Lady Madeline murmured. "Do *try* to make an effort."

"If I may have your attention?" Whitborough's voice rang out across the ballroom. "We'd like to thank all of you for coming and for being part of our celebration. Tonight marks a momentous occasion for both of our families, as we announce the betrothal of our son Harold, Earl of Denforth, to Lady Margaret Carlisle."

"A match that has been long in the making," the Duke of Langdale added, with his gentle, rather unworldly smile. "But my duchess and I could not be more pleased than to see our daughter joined in marriage to the son of our oldest friends."

Whitborough returned his smile. "Nor Her Grace and myself, to welcome this lovely young woman into our family! And so tonight," the duke paused to accept a flute of champagne, then raised it high, "I propose a toast to the newly betrothed couple and their bright future! Lord Denforth and Lady Margaret!"

"Lord Denforth and Lady Margaret!" the assembled guests echoed, and drank.

❄

WITH THE ANNOUNCEMENT DULY MADE, the musicians struck up a quadrille from the gallery, and the dancing began. As expected, Hal led Margaret out onto the floor. The light from the chandelier illuminated his bright hair and even brighter smile. Only someone who knew him well—from the cradle on, for example—would have detected that his smile didn't reach his eyes.

Oh, Hal. A fierce surge of love for her twin swept over Madeline: love tinged with fear, a fear that she knew was shared by everyone who cared for him. So handsome, so dashing, so debonair, and at the same time, so *lost*. Two years ago, he'd tried to assert himself by laying claim to real power—and failed. Now he drifted aimlessly from pleasure to pleasure, with nothing to anchor him. If he could only *see* how much he might benefit from the steadfast love and faith of a girl like Margaret, who would do anything to please him...

A familiar voice spoke her name, and she turned to find Jack Middleton—her partner for the quadrille—holding out his hand. Accepting it, she let him lead her onto the floor. Lord Saxby, she noticed, was escorting Olivia Middleton, and her estimation of him rose further still when she saw her friend's smile. Most men tended to overlook Olivia in favor of Christabel, and while the former professed not to mind, she would have to be a saint not to resent it now and then. And to relish the times when she was noticed and appreciated.

Fortunately, no lady was destined to be a wallflower tonight, unless it was by choice. Even with the additional guests, the men outnumbered the women, so there was no shortage of partners. Most of Madeline's dances had been spoken for, and she enjoyed them all, even as her mind insisted on racing ahead to the moment Lord Saxby would come to claim her.

Her heart bounded in her chest when she saw him

approach, and she gave him her most brilliant smile in greeting. "Lord Saxby! *God match me with a good dancer!*"

He smiled back, his eyes crinkling irresistibly. "Well, my sisters tell me I'm passable, and I haven't stepped on a lady's toes in years. Will that do?"

Madeline made a show of looking him up and down. "It might. Shall we?"

They joined the other couples assembling on the dance floor, took up their place in the set: Madeline's pulse quickened at the sensation of Lord Saxby's right hand at her waist, its warmth perceivable even through his glove and the silk of her gown. His other hand held hers in a light but firm clasp. The music began—"The Artist's Life," one of Madeline's favorite Strauss waltzes —and Lord Saxby guided her into a graceful opening turn.

It shouldn't have surprised her that he danced well, moving with the same confidence and assurance he brought to the sports he loved. More than that, Madeline felt safe—cherished, even—in his arms. She knew herself to be tall for a woman, yet dancing with Lord Saxby made her feel almost petite. To say nothing of the way his proximity affected her. The intimacy of the waltz could be a mixed blessing, but tonight she welcomed it, breathing in the lemony scent of his cologne and savoring the warmth of the strong, athletic frame so close to hers.

One more night. Madeline could hardly bear to think about the morning—and his looming departure. But he wouldn't be the honorable man she believed him to be if he did not honor his previous engagement. She had to trust that he too felt the attraction between them, that she was not merely imagining the light in his eyes when he looked at her, and that he *would* be back... just as he'd said he might.

He turned her again, so lightly and deftly, that she was scarcely conscious of it, because her whole world had narrowed to his eyes, his smile, his encircling arm. Ten days ago, she'd considered only that she might discover a few potential suitors among their guests, men whose company she might enjoy and with whom she could imagine herself spending more time. She'd never expected to form an attachment—much less, one this strong—so quickly. A miracle... but Christmastide wasn't only the season of miracles, but the season of faith. She *would* have faith, in him and in them.

She smiled up at him, letting all her faith—and hope—shine through, and thought she heard his breath catch. The music faded into silence and the whirling couples slowed and stopped, many gazing raptly into each other's eyes. As she and Saxby were doing.

He was the one to speak first, his voice husky, almost tentative. "Lady Madeline, would you care for some refreshment now? Or are you bespoken for the next dance?"

She shook her head. "I left some of my dances unclaimed, Lord Saxby. Just in case, I should want a respite, after." A respite with *you*. "But I don't require refreshment at the moment. Perhaps we might—go for a walk instead?"

"Ah." He paused, then added with commendable swiftness, "As it happens, I've heard much about the beauty of Denforth's conservatory. Might I prevail upon you to show it to me?"

"You may indeed, Lord Saxby."

❅

ONE LAST NIGHT, Hugo thought with a pang as he escorted Lady Madeline discreetly from the ballroom. He could reckon their remaining time together in hours. *Best make the most of each moment, then.*

Achieving the doorway, they slipped into the passage—and started guiltily when a voice spoke from the shadows.

"Avoiding the crush? Can't say I blame you. Found *I* needed some air myself."

Denforth, glass in hand, was slouched with careless elegance against a wall. His betrothed was nowhere in sight, Hugo observed.

As did Lady Madeline, her gaze going from startled to mildly disapproving. "Hal, where's Margaret? It's your engagement party—you really should be with her."

"Managing Maddie." Denforth took a healthy swallow of something considerably darker—and likely more potent—than champagne. "You needn't worry about my intended. She's currently dancing with one of the Middletons. Besides, I'll have the rest of my life to be with Margaret. Eons, no doubt. Just as our fathers have decreed."

Hugo blinked, taken aback by the faint but unmistakable bitterness in the younger man's tone. And by the tug of pity he experienced for him—and more acutely, for his new fiancée.

"You never objected to the match before," Lady Madeline reminded her brother.

He shrugged. "Wouldn't have done any good if I had. Those whom Whitborough and Langdale hath joined together, let no man put asunder."

"If you'd formed an attachment to someone just as suitable—"

"Why the devil must I form any sort of 'attachment' at all?" Denforth demanded peevishly, a scowl marring his handsome face. "A woman may be on the shelf at twenty-three, but it's just the *start* of life for a man!"

"Thank you so much for the reminder," his sister said dryly.

"Just because Father married young, why should the rest of us?" Denforth went on, as though she hadn't spoken. "*You're* taking your time about it, aren't you?"

Lady Madeline stiffened, but held on to her composure—with an iron grip, Hugo suspected. "I have my reasons."

"You always do. Enjoy the party." Denforth toasted them with his glass. "Someone should, at any rate," he added, not quite under his breath. "Now, if you'll excuse me, I hear a deck of cards calling my name."

Ignoring his sister's disapproving stare, he tossed back his drink and strolled away.

"Your brother doesn't seem exactly overjoyed by his new status," Hugo remarked.

"He'll come to terms with it—eventually. And she'll be good for him," Lady Madeline insisted. "Even if he can't see it yet. Margaret has a sound head on her shoulders. A lot of common sense. If anyone can steady Hal—"

It seemed a heavy burden to settle upon the shoulders of a seventeen-year-old girl, Hugo reflected. Not to mention that Denforth seemed disinclined to pay his new fiancée much heed, whereas Lady Margaret clearly worshipped him. Silently, he wished the betrothed couple good luck—he had the feeling they were going to need it.

Lady Madeline shook her head as though trying to dislodge unpleasant thoughts. "Shall we go on, Lord Saxby? The conservatory's not far from here."

They proceeded along the passage, rounded a corner, then she opened a many-paned glass door and they stepped into spring. Or so it felt to Hugo, as he breathed in mild, soft air scented with jasmine, citrus, and countless other, less identifiable fragrances.

"This is *Maman*'s favorite place in winter. And one of mine, as well," Lady Madeline told him.

"I can see why." Looking around, Hugo spied a few lanterns bobbing gently overhead, illuminating the shrubs, flowers, and paved walkways. After the crowded, noisy ballroom, the conservatory was a haven of soft shadows and cloistered quiet. Arm in arm, they strolled along the nearest path, content merely to be in each other's company.

Then an eerie wail shattered the silence, building to a crescendo fit to raise the hair on the back of one's neck. Lady Madeline flinched and drew just a little closer to Hugo.

"*The isle is full of noises.*" The quotation from *The Tempest* popped into his head; he saw her lips twitch in appreciation. But before she could respond, another human voice succeeded the cacophony.

"*Sweet Moon, I thank thee for thy sunny beams / I thank thee, Moon, for shining now so bright.*" Shakespeare again, recited with effortless ease, though with a somewhat pixilated air.

Hugo darted a questioning glance at Lady Madeline who had relaxed visibly, though her brows were knit in a faint, puzzled frown. She motioned to Hugo, and they ventured towards the voice, which had come from just ahead of them on the path.

Lord Gervase was sitting on a stone bench, his head tipped up towards the night sky and the winter moon casting its pale radiance through the glass panels. A black cat—the most likely source of that unearthly cry—

occupied the other end of the bench, its head also canted skyward.

As Hugo and Lady Madeline approached, the cat hissed, leapt down from the bench, and vanished into the shrubbery. Lord Gervase only turned his head, waggled his fingers in a brief wave, before shifting his gaze back to the moon and continuing his recital, *"For by thy gracious, golden, glittering gleams—"*

Lady Madeline's eyes widened as she spotted the glass and half-empty decanter on the bench beside her brother. "Gervase, you're—you're *drunk!*"

She'd shown disapproval rather than surprise over Denforth imbibing. But the shock in her voice now was palpable, as if the Apocalypse were imminent. Hugo felt nearly as taken aback: of all the Lyons brothers, he'd have reckoned Lord Gervase the least likely to indulge in this sort of excess.

The younger man's eyes glittered in the shadows, almost feverishly bright. "Very astute of you, sister mine. *Today it is our pleasure to be drunk, / And this our queen shall be as drunk as we.*"

"But why?" Lady Madeline sounded genuinely perplexed.

Lord Gervase spread his hands wide in an expansive gesture. "Is not tonight a joyous occasion? A ducal engagement: the winter of our discontent made glorious summer by this son of Whitborough! Wait," he paused, frowning, "that doesn't rhyme, does it? Or scan. Oh, well—one can't have everything. As I have cause to know." Picking up his glass, he squinted at the contents. *"Well, here's my comfort!"*

"Ger, hadn't you better stop? You'll have an awful head in the morning."

He gave her a brilliant, wavering smile, but continued to hold his glass aloft. "I propose a toast. *All for love, and a little for the bottle.*"

Light footsteps pattered behind them, they turned to see Lady Elaine approaching, her pretty face creased with concern. "Ah, there you are, Ger! I've been looking for you."

"Elaine the fair, Elaine the loveable..." Lord Gervase turned his overbright gaze on her now. *"Comfort me with apples, stay me with flagons. For I am sick of love."*

"I think you've had enough flagons for the night. Why don't we go upstairs now? You'll be the better for some sleep." Lady Elaine spoke gently, but firmly, sounding for all the world as though *she* were the elder of the two. In her ivory gown, bleached by the moonlight, she looked almost ethereal, an angel sent down from heaven to minister to fools and drunkards.

Their eyes locked, and to Hugo's astonishment, Lord Gervase was the first to look away, setting his glass down on the bench with exaggerated care before taking Lady Elaine's outstretched hand. Once on his feet, he swayed and she moved closer to steady him.

Lord Gervase closed his eyes, swallowing hard. "I prithee, do not spin me round and round. *My stomach is not constant.*"

Hugo and Lady Madeline both took a precautionary step back.

"No one is spinning you, Ger," Lady Elaine said patiently. "Here, lean on me, and we'll make it to your chamber just fine."

"Better you than me," Hugo heard Lady Madeline murmur under her breath.

Lord Gervase cracked his eyes open. "I should—summon a footman to help," he said, sounding a fraction more coherent. "An' *you* should go back to the ballroom, Lainey."

She shook her head, guiding him a few steps along the path. "That would take too long."

"Don't—want to disgrace myself on your gown..."

"I have other gowns. I have only one favorite brother."

Lord Gervase absorbed this for a moment. "I didn't know I was *anyone's* favorite."

The words sounded unbearably stark. Hugo heard Lady Madeline catch her breath, but Lady Elaine never missed a beat.

"Well, now you know," she said hardily, shooting her sister and Hugo a warning glance. "I wouldn't do this for just anyone, after all."

A corner of Lord Gervase's mouth crooked up, but he seemed reassured by Lady Elaine's remark and said nothing more as she led him from the conservatory.

Hugo stared after them, bemused. The three things

that had struck him most about Lord Gervase were his intelligence, his independence, and his detachment. And now the mask had slipped—at least, with regard to the last. Sliding his gaze over to Lady Madeline, he saw that she looked as bewildered as he felt. Bewildered and troubled, her eyes so dark a green they appeared almost black in the dimly-lit conservatory.

"Lord Gervase doesn't seem the sort to drink to excess," he ventured at last.

Lady Madeline bit her lip. "He's not. I don't know what's got into him tonight."

"Apart from the brandy, you mean?"

His attempt to lighten the mood fell flat; the distress on her face only deepened. "What he said, about not being anyone's favorite. I never knew that..." Her voice trailed off helplessly.

"That he saw things that way?"

"That he *minded*." She paused, then said in a voice consciously devoid of emotion, "Hal has been the apple of my father's eye, practically from the moment he was born."

"It's not uncommon for the title holder to prefer the heir. Not *fair*, but not uncommon."

"And my mother dotes on Reg," she continued with the same chill precision. "Neither of my parents troubles to disguise their partiality, *or* to curb the rivalry that stems from it. Just one of the *many* reasons the Lyons family falls woefully short of perfection."

"Most families do," he pointed out. "I can't think of a single one that measures up to such a standard, including my own."

"Understanding that in one's head and accepting it in one's heart are two different things—especially when you're a child." Her lips formed a bittersweet smile. "When I was growing up, I thought *my* family was special. Extraordinary."

He reached for her hand; even through her glove, it felt cold in his. "They are. Even on short acquaintance I can see that."

She lowered her gaze, stared at the ground. "And my father... he was my idol. Then just before I came out, I learned he had a mistress. And that *Maman* knew."

Hugo winced. Between Branscombe and Charley,

he'd picked up more than a few choice details about the Whitboroughs' oft-tempestuous marriage, but he could only imagine what it must have been like to live in such an atmosphere. And for a girl who'd adored her father... "I'm sorry. That would be a damnable time to make such a discovery. Not that there's a *good* time for it," he added hastily.

"I brazened it out my entire first Season. Pretended that all was well, and that our family was happy, united, and whole. My performance as Lady Capulet was nothing compared to my portrayal of a devoted daughter." Her haunted eyes lifted to his. "But inside..."

"You must have been deeply hurt. And angry."

Lady Madeline nodded tightly. "I couldn't believe he'd betray *Maman*—that he'd betray *all* of us. I couldn't understand why we weren't enough for him. Why he'd risk *our* family, everything we had, for *her*." She paused, swallowing hard. "She died last winter, of some ailment of the lung. Then he and *Maman* reconciled this past spring—and I've found that every bit as hard to accept as his original betrayal."

Forgive those who trespass against us. So much easier said than done, Hugo thought.

Pain shimmered in her eyes as words continued to tumble out of her. "If I could just forgive him, as my mother seems to have done—or hate him completely, it would be so much easier! As it is, I can hardly bear to be in his presence anymore. Every time I see him, I remember that year, and how much it *hurt*..."

The desolation in her eyes, in her voice, moved him more than tears. "Oh, my dear."

It felt like the most natural thing in the world, then, to put his arm around her as he might have around one of his sisters. She turned blindly in his embrace, almost burrowing against him, seeking warmth, comfort... and something more, as her cheek brushed against his, and the world contracted to shared breaths, shared heartbeats, and the scent of roses and neroli.

Desire crashed over Hugo like a wave, sweeping him from his moorings. Drawing her closer, he sought the lips hovering so close to his own. Sought and claimed them, tenderly at first, then with a mounting hunger that she matched, kissing him as eagerly as he was kissing her, winding her arms about his neck in a fierce embrace. His free hand cupped the back of her head, his fingers tangling in the silk of her hair. *Never before have I kissed a woman in a moonlit conservatory...*

They finally pulled away, breathless and shaken. In the moonlight, Lady Madeline's eyes were now the color of storm-tossed seas, brilliant and turbulent at once.

"*You kiss by the book.*" Her voice was husky, edged with wondering laughter as she fingered her slightly swollen lips.

O trespass sweetly urged! Dazed, Hugo put up a hand, brushed a straying dark curl back from her brow. "Lady Madeline—"

"Don't you dare apologize, Lord Saxby," she broke in, her eyes still luminous. "This has been far and away the high point of my evening."

He found himself smiling, ridiculously pleased by her assertion. "Thank you for the compliment. But I think... we should go back to the ballroom now."

"Must we?"

Wistfulness colored her tone, and Hugo fought the urge to pull her into his arms again and let the rest of the world go hang. Mastering that urge he inquired gently, "Doesn't Falstaff say something about discretion being the better part of valor?"

She sighed, conceding his point. "Best not to risk a scandal, I suppose."

"My thoughts exactly." Hugo offered his arm. "But just so you know," he added, "this has been the high point of *my* evening as well."

Her answering smile outshone the stars.

THE BALL WAS STILL in full swing when they reentered the salon, with couples prancing across the floor to the strains of a lively polka. Glancing about the room, Hugo spied the Whitboroughs deep in conversation with the Langdales—and Lady Margaret. The girl's smile was resolute, but Hugo thought he detected a hint of strain about her eyes. Denforth remained conspicuous by his absence.

"There's Lainey," Lady Madeline said suddenly, her hand tightening on Hugo's arm.

Following her gaze, he saw that Lady Elaine had indeed re-entered the ballroom. She still wore her ivory gown, which suggested that she'd got Lord Gervase upstairs without mishap.

Lady Madeline fretted her lower lip. "Lord Saxby, I'd like—to have a private word with my sister, if you don't mind."

About their brother, Hugo suspected. And Lady Elaine would almost certainly reveal more without a stranger present.

"Why don't I go to the supper room and bring back some refreshment?" he offered. "A glass of lemonade, perhaps, unless you'd prefer champagne?"

She flashed him a quick, grateful smile. "Lemonade would be lovely. I think perhaps the wine has flowed a bit *too* freely tonight."

"Good point," Hugo agreed. "I'll be back —presently."

Entering the supper room, he was surprised to see a familiar figure standing by the punch bowl, ladling out a glass of lemonade.

"Good evening, Wilf. Fetching refreshment for Miss Christabel, are you?" It certainly hadn't escaped Hugo's notice that, ever since the hunt, his brother had spent more time in her company than in Denforth's.

His brother flushed, but a decidedly moonstruck smile played about his mouth. "Dancing is thirsty work, she tells me."

Picking up a glass, Hugo joined him at the punch bowl. "When a lady dances as well as she does, she certainly won't lack for partners."

Wilf's eyes lit up. "She *is* rather marvelous, isn't she?"

"Very pretty and every inch a lady," Hugo agreed, smiling too. "Should I be asking you your intentions towards her?"

He spoke half in jest—and was astonished to see Wilf's flush deepen and a speculative gleam kindle in his eyes. Good God, was his baby brother actually contemplating *marriage*?

"Hugo," Wilf began diffidently, "if I *were* to—pay my

addresses to Christabel, do you think Sir George would look kindly on my suit?"

No question but he was in earnest. And thus deserved a serious reply.

"I do not know Sir George Middleton well," Hugo said, after a moment. "But I think his foremost concern would be how you mean to support a wife and later, a family. What your plans for the future might be, and how you are currently situated."

Wilf absorbed this in silence, but he looked thoughtful, rather than discouraged—or fearful, which spoke volumes about the nature of this growing attachment. And certainly Miss Christabel could do much worse than the second son of the Earl of Bevington, Hugo decided. "However, Father and I could provide him with a clearer picture of your prospects, which are not inconsiderable," he added and saw Wilf's face brighten. "And Sir George strikes me as a reasonable man. So, if your liking is reciprocated, *and* if there is no other serious contender in the offing—"

"There isn't!" Wilf broke in. "Not yet, at least!"

"Then I see no reason why he wouldn't consent to your courtship," Hugo finished. "Indeed, I think he would be fortunate to have you for a son-in-law."

His brother exhaled in obvious relief, his eyes fairly blazing. "Thanks, Hugo! I can't tell you how much it means to hear that from you!"

Hugo clapped him lightly on the shoulder. "I'm pleased to see that your choice has lighted on such a worthy young woman. But bear in mind that she is quite young," he warned. "And so are you, having just attained your majority. If Sir George consents, you still might have to endure a lengthy engagement."

"Oh, I don't mind that!" Wilf declared ebulliently. "I know I have to prove myself to him, first But I'll wait as long as I have to—because Christabel is worth it."

The conviction in his voice rang like a bell, and Hugo regarded him with something close to awe. Almost overnight, it seemed, his younger brother had become a man. Who'd have imagined that a baronet's dark-eyed daughter could have wrought such a transformation? At the same time he experienced a twinge of what might have been envy: that Wilf could know this soon, this clearly, that only one woman would do...

Unexpectedly, his brother asked, "And what of your affairs, Hugo? Do they prosper?"

"*My* affairs?" he echoed, caught off-guard by the question.

Wilf shook his head, almost indulgently. "I'm not blind, you know! It's plain to see that *you* fancy Lady Madeline!"

"I find her to be a very attractive and amusing young woman—"

"Judging from the way you look at her, *I* think you find her much more than that!"

Hugo regarded his brother narrowly. "Do you?"

"Yes, and in my opinion, she's just what you need!" Wilf retorted. "She's clever, lively, and fun! *Much* more interesting than that Lady Althea Charley told me you've been courting!"

A slight noise behind them drew their attention to the doorway.

Where Lady Madeline was now standing, her face colorless and completely without expression. For one soul-freezing moment, her eyes met Hugo's, then she was gone in a whirl of rose-colored skirts.

Damnation! Hastily setting down his glass, Hugo followed.

HE OVERTOOK her in the passage, catching hold of her nearest wrist. "Madeline, for God's sake, wait!"

She stiffened at his touch. "Let go of my arm, Lord Saxby." Every syllable sounded as though it had been chipped from ice.

He tightened his grip instead. "Not until you hear what I have to say!"

She would not look at him but stared resolutely ahead. "What is left to say? You are engaged—to Lady Althea Clement, I surmise."

"*No.* Not engaged, or even promised, I swear!"

"What is she to you, then?"

Hugo swallowed, desperately searching for the right words. "I spent some time in her company this Season, and wondered...if she and I might suit." Wondered, had been almost convinced of it—until this past week had changed everything. Until *this* woman's vivid, vibrant reality had rendered the other as pale and insubstantial as a dream, by comparison.

Lady Madeline stilled. "I know her, a little. She is pretty, well-dowered, and of impeccable birth and breeding. An excellent choice for a future countess."

So Hugo had told himself barely a fortnight ago. Dear God, how fatuous he had been—and how *blind!* "Lady Madeline—"

"I suppose you're expected at the Clements' for Christmas?" she inquired, as though he hadn't spoken.

"I am, but—"

"Then, by all means, you must go. *Honor* demands that you keep your appointment. And Lady Althea," she turned to look at him at last, her eyes tearless but impenetrably dark in her white face, "may yet have hopes of you, raised by your previous attentions to her."

He swallowed again, shame and guilt churning in his stomach. "On my word of honor, Lady Madeline—as little as you may regard it now—I was not *bound* to anyone when I came to Yorkshire!"

"Does the lady you were courting *before* coming here feel the same?" she countered sharply. "That neither of you are bound, and therefore free to—*amuse* yourselves with someone else? To indulge in some holiday frolic, of no lasting consequence?"

"Never that!" he exclaimed, appalled. "Good God, do you think me so shallow, so contemptible, that I would trifle with *you*, of all women?"

She closed her eyes, her face as desolate as he'd seen it in the conservatory. "I don't know what to think of you anymore."

The bleakness in her voice seared him to the soul. Of course she distrusted him now—she who had been so deeply hurt by Whitborough's infidelity and who must be wondering if *he* were cut from the same faithless cloth.

Never before have I broken someone's heart. And never before have I felt like such a cad.

"Madeline." Her name was feather-light upon his

tongue. "Maddie... I swear that I meant every word I said to you, tonight and every other night."

She opened her eyes and he saw the warring emotions there before she turned away again. "I believe you, Lord Saxby. Just as I believe that you meant everything you said to Lady Althea too." The faint tremor in her voice was almost undetectable. "I pray you will excuse me from our second dance. I find myself—indisposed."

The arm Hugo held felt as inert and unresponsive as a statue's. Miserably, he released her and stepped back. In desperation, he mounted one last defense. "My dear, I know I've handled things badly, but I swear I'll make them right, if you just give me the chance!"

"*Do not swear and eat it.* Good night, Lord Saxby."

Sparing him not a glance, Lady Madeline straightened to her full height and walked away. The light, the color, and the warmth all went with her, leaving him in the shadows.

Chapter Six

> *How like a winter hath my absence been*
> *From thee, the pleasure of the fleeting year!*
> *What freezings have I felt, what dark days*
> *   seen!*
> *What old December's bareness everywhere!*
> —WILLIAM SHAKESPEARE, *Sonnet XCVII*

Yorkshire, 28 December 1879

"*SO FAIR AND FOUL a day I have not seen.*"

Quoting from *Macbeth* might be tempting fate, but Madeline felt cross-grained enough to risk it. Still, according to superstition, it was only inside of a theatre that one should avoid doing so, and she was outside and mounted on Juno for a morning ride.

Besides, no other play happened to match her mood at present. The day was surprisingly pleasant: a mild winter sun shone overhead, making the light dusting of snow on the ground sparkle like powdered diamonds. Within Madeline's heart, however, a storm continued to rage.

Slowing Juno to a walk, she bleakly contemplated the last week. Christmas had come and gone, along with the St. Stephen's Day hunt. But there had been no blond, broad-shouldered Hector galloping across the fields, dazzling her with his horsemanship and the sight of him in riding dress. She'd told herself repeatedly to forget him, that there were other fish in the sea, but the empty place where he'd been felt as obvious as a missing tooth—and ached far more.

She'd been a fool not to suspect that there might be someone else he was courting. And twice a fool to let herself fall—in love? Her cheeks flamed when she remembered the way she'd confided in him, all the things she'd said that night in the conservatory. And that kiss...

I'll make things right, if you just give me the chance! His words still rang in her ears, and she was no doubt three times a fool for wanting desperately to believe him. For hoping every day since his departure that he'd come striding through the front door—this time, to stay. As it was, her heart leapt into her throat every time she heard a carriage pull up before the house, only to sink like a stone when someone else emerged from it. Finally, disgusted with her maudlin mood, she'd fled the house for the outdoors and the soothing presence of her mare.

Unfortunately, memories of Lord Saxby accompanied her. Was he even now at the Clements', sitting by the fire with pretty, proper Lady Althea? Listening to her with the same rapt attention he'd shown Madeline just a week ago? Smiling at her with that frank admiration in his eyes? Or worse, was he closeted with Lord Clement, discussing marriage settlements, pin money, and dowries?

Madeline's heart clenched at the thought. She should be furious with Lord Saxby, should never want to lay eyes on him again after his deceit, and yet... a traitorous voice in her head insisted that he had never *intended* to deceive, that he'd spoken truly about there being no formal engagement between him and Lady Althea. And when he told her he'd meant everything he said to her.

Her mother had somehow managed to forgive her father for his infidelity, for an affair that had lasted several years. What Lord Saxby had done was nowhere near as bad: was he beyond forgiveness? And if he *were* to return, should she give him another chance?

But if thou meanest not well, I do beseech thee... To cease thy suit and leave me to my grief. Juliet again. Madeline found herself with a degree of sympathy for the ill-fated Miss Capulet that she hadn't experienced since *she* was fourteen!

The pounding of horse's hooves roused her from her

thoughts. Glancing toward the sound, she saw a lone rider approaching, astride a handsome bay hunter who bore a strong resemblance to Lysander...

She looked again—sharply—at the rider this time. A tall, broad-shouldered man in a black Melton coat that emphasized his athletic form. The hair beneath his high-crowned hat was fair, curling over a noble brow, and his gaze was frank and open.

He reined in Lysander—it *was* Lysander—within a few feet of her, and they stared uncertainly at each other. His smile was absent, she noticed, and there was the faintest of creases between his brows. Indeed, he appeared unwontedly serious and almost tentative, as though unsure of his welcome. *As he should be*, the voice in Madeline's head observed tartly.

It took several tries to force words past the constriction in her throat. "Lord Saxby. You've missed the hunt, I'm afraid."

THE COMMONPLACE WORDS, along with her matter-of-fact tone, eased the tension. Only a fraction, but Hugo was prepared to take what he could get.

"I didn't come for the hunt, Lady Madeline," he replied, holding her gaze steadily. She wasn't the sort to go into a decline over a man, but he thought she looked a trifle paler than he remembered, even with the winter chill deepening the color in her cheeks.

She looked away, as though suddenly fascinated by the scenery around them. "Am I to wish you happy, then —you and Lady Althea?"

"I am sure Lady Althea *will* be made happy, sooner rather than later—but not by me."

She flicked a sideways glance at him. "No? But she is suitable for you, in every way. Moreover, I've heard the Clements are among the most well-behaved families in England, and their country seat—Southwood, I believe? —is accounted one of the prettiest."

Her cool composure irked him, though he couldn't blame her for holding him at arm's length. After the way they'd parted, he could hardly expect her to fall into his arms the moment she saw him again. Still, two could play at this game. "Correct on both counts. The estate is handsome, and my hosts were nothing if not hospitable."

Lady Madeline's lips compressed, but she managed a polite nod. "I am glad to hear it, Lord Saxby."

"Hampshire is beautiful country—well worth visiting," Hugo went on. "And the weather was remarkably mild, for winter."

"Mild," in fact, summed up his entire stay with the Clements, he reflected. Even the festivities had had a muted air about them: evenings singing carols about the piano or playing cards or backgammon. No Charades— Lady Clement considered the game too frivolous—or amateur theatricals. Not even a Nativity tableau. Aloud, he said, "They keep Christmas quietly at Southwood. And the whole family agrees very happily together. I don't believe I heard a single cross word between them while I was there."

Lady Madeline fretted her lip—the first sign of perturbation he'd seen. "None at all? How singular."

"No rows, no rivalries, no spats—not even between the sons. Lady Althea has two older brothers, and I gather they're the best of friends."

"Even more extraordinary." She was staring resolutely down at her horse's reins.

"Her sister, Lady Prunella, is a model of decorum, even at twelve," Hugo continued. "Obeys her governess, only speaks when spoken to. One cannot imagine her roaming through passages in search of missing cats. Or concerning herself with the fate of a litter of kittens."

She looked up at that, a spark in her changeable eyes. "No? Well, forgive my candor, Lord Saxby, but *I* would not trade our Juliana for such a one, were she ten times as decorous!"

And there was *his* Madeline, after all. "Nor would I," Hugo agreed affably. "The plain truth is, I found the lot of them as placid and unexcitable as a herd of cows. Not that I've anything against cows, but as companions, they can be... rather less than stimulating."

He paused, smiling into her astonished eyes. "The whole time I was there, surrounded by peace, tranquility, and good will towards men, the most absurd questions kept popping into my mind—at the most inconvenient moments! Had you found homes for all the kittens yet?

Were Denforth and Lord Reginald still competing over every little thing? Why did your brother Gervase get drunk the night of the ball? And most important of all, was someone else watching the snow fall with you, and kissing you in the conservatory?"

She caught her breath, but rallied quickly. "To answer your questions: we're keeping the last two kittens, Hal and Reg wagered yesterday on the outcome of a billiards match that lasted more than an hour, and Ger claims to remember nothing whatsoever about that night. And as to the last," her color rose, but her gaze did not waver, "I would have to say no, to both."

"That's good to know. Otherwise, I might have to tear the fellow limb from limb, which would be a poor way to end the old year, or begin the new."

Her brows arched. "Good heavens, my lord! Is Lady Althea aware of your violent tendencies?"

"No, but she *is* now aware of something far more important: that, while I admire and esteem her, my heart is no longer free to give. Because I left it behind, in Yorkshire. Much to my relief, she bore the news with equanimity—and bade me go in search of it." Hugo took a breath, steeling himself for what was to come. "And so I have. I only hope that I may be allowed to retrieve it. Or better yet, that I may ask for yours in return—along with your hand."

He thought he saw elation flare in her eyes, before they cooled to wariness again. "Do you truly believe that we would suit?"

"I do now," he replied staunchly. "Before I came here, my sister Charley told me that I needed 'stirring up.' That I'd become settled and staid before my time— mainly because of our father's accident. He was crippled more than a dozen years ago, when his carriage overturned going down a hill."

Her expression softened at once. "I'm sorry. I didn't know."

"Father needed me to take on more responsibility, to become his right hand. I was only sixteen at the time, but I was glad to help in any way I could. I was the heir, after all—duty-bound to do the right thing by the estate and our family. Which included choosing a future countess, when the time came," he added with a wry smile.

"Lady Althea met all the requirements for the position, and I expected we would be content together. I convinced myself that that would be enough. And then I met *you*—and it was like seeing the world afresh, through a flash of lightning."

"The *coup de foudre*," she murmured, her voice barely audible.

"Just so. As it turns out, my irritating sister was right. I don't need a proper, placid bride who'll accommodate me. I need one who will push me, challenge me, and jolt me out of my complacency, if necessary. As you have—from the very start. Because of you, I've done things that it would never have occurred to me even to try." He leaned forward in the saddle, his gaze locking with hers. "Never before have I... let myself fall deeply in love. Never before have I asked a woman to marry me. And never before has so much depended on her answer."

Her eyes shone brilliant green in the winter sunlight, like the promise of spring to come. "Lord Saxby... you're in good company, as it turns out. Never before have *I* told a man—outside of my family—that I care for him."

"Only 'care'?" he queried gently.

Her color deepened. "Oh, very well—'*love*'! Never before have I been tempted by an offer of marriage. And never before have I said yes. Until this moment."

"Then—it's 'yes'?"

She smiled then, a transcendent smile like the one he'd seen that night in the conservatory and carried in his heart since their parting. "Yes."

Joy blazed through him, burning away all the fears and uncertainties. Kneeing Lysander forward, he drew level with her, reached out to cup her cheek. Pliant as a willow, she leaned into his embrace, her lips seeking his.

The first time either of them had kissed while on horseback.

But far from the last.

Epilogue

❦

At Christmas play and make good cheer,
For Christmas comes but once a year.
—THOMAS TUSSER, *A Hundred Good Points*
  of Husbandry

Yorkshire, 23 December 1880

"FOR GOD'S SAKE, MADDIE! Come down from there at once and bring Baby with you!"

Securing the dangling end of the garland over the mantelpiece, Madeline smiled indulgently at Hugo before descending from the stool into his protective embrace. "In case you hadn't noticed, darling, Baby and I are inseparable—for the next five months, anyway. And there's no need to fuss. I was mere inches off the ground and never in any danger of falling."

"Accidents can happen," Hugo pointed out, resting a hand lightly on her abdomen. At four months forward, her pregnancy was just beginning to show, a gentle curve that he found every bit as arousing as her willow-wand slenderness before their wedding. "Eight months married and you're *still* stopping my heart. Heaven help me if our daughter is just like you!"

"I might be having a boy," she reminded him.

"True, but I've a fancy for a girl—though either would be welcome," he added hastily.

The Whitboroughs were delighted at the prospect of their first grandchild, as were Hugo's parents. The latter had been surprised by his choice of bride at first, but much to his relief, they'd quickly warmed to Madeline, especially when she conceived soon after the wedding. Charley, Victoria, and Wilf also approved, all declaring that she was exactly what their eldest brother needed.

Hugo had been a little nervous about his reception by his formidable in-laws. Fortunately, the Whitboroughs had welcomed him to the family: doubtless because of his sterling qualities *and* his willingness to take their eldest daughter off their hands, Madeline had observed wryly.

"I refuse to hear such slanders about my future wife," Hugo had retorted, kissing her soundly. "Besides, their loss is *my* gain!"

Madeline's siblings had also accepted him without reservation, and Hugo had grown fond of each and every one of them, and not only for Madeline's sake. However contentious and quarrelsome they were as a family, he couldn't help liking them as individuals.

And they had all gathered here this afternoon in the Great Hall to decorate the Christmas tree, already glittering with tinsel and fully seven feet high. Madeline's sisters. Hal and Reg—he could call them that, now, though it had taken some adjustment on his part. The Langdales and their children; Lady Margaret—taller and prettier—was still deeply smitten with Hal, who continued to treat her with the careless kindness of an older brother. Young Jason. Elaine had even managed to drag Gervase down from his chamber for this.

And at the center of the festivities, the Duke and Duchess of Whitborough, the latter sitting with a carved wooden chest upon her lap. As Hugo glanced in her direction, she smiled and beckoned to him.

"*Mon beau-fils*, I have something for you."

Curious, his arm still firmly about his wife, he went over to her. Opening the chest, Her Grace held it out to him, revealing a tray filled with beautiful, handmade ornaments in every conceivable color and shape.

"I welcomed you to the family on Madeline's wedding day, my dear," his mother-in-law began. "This just makes it *more* official." She indicated a dark blue ornament, oblong, with his first initial—stitched in gold thread—on one side and a gold tassel dangling from its end. "Happy Christmas, *chéri*."

"Come and hang it," Madeline invited, smiling as she reached into the chest and took out a rose and silver ornament marked with an *M*. "Right next to mine."

More moved than he dared admit, Hugo kissed Her Grace on the cheek, then took up his ornament and did as his wife suggested, placing it on a bough adjacent to the one she chose.

"Well done!" Whitborough declared heartily, and a murmur of assent rippled through the Great Hall.

One by one, the Lyons family hung their ornaments on the tree, then as a finishing touch. Hal climbed the ladder and placed an intricate crystal star on the top. Descending carefully, he stepped back with the rest of them to admire their handiwork.

"I think it's the best tree we've ever had!" Juliana exclaimed, gazing raptly up at it.

The duchess rested a hand on her daughter's bright head. "You may be right, *petite*."

Looking up at the shimmering star, Hugo caught sight of something else almost directly overhead: something white and green, secured to the branches of the chandelier by dangling scarlet ribbons.

"Another first, my love," he remarked to Madeline, nestling in the circle of his arm.

"Never before have you received your very own Christmas ornament?" she queried, smiling up at him.

"That goes without saying. I was about to observe that never before have I kissed my wife under the mistletoe. And now seems like an excellent time to start."

And with that, Hugo proceeded to suit the action to the word.

Thank You

Thank you for reading *The Advent of Lady Madeline*, the prequel novella in my new series, **The Lyons Pride**! I hope you enjoyed it.

Would you like to know when my next book is available? You can find out by signing up for my newsletter at my website at http://www.pamelasherwood.com. Or follow me on Twitter at https://twitter.com/pamela_sherwood or like my Facebook Page at https://www.facebook.com/PamelaSherwoodAuthor.

Reviews help readers find books, so I hope you will consider leaving a review at your venue of choice. I appreciate all reviews, whether positive or negative.

Lord Gervase Lyons is the hero of *Devices & Desires*—the first full-length novel in the series. A young man of wit, intellect, and ambition, Gervase harbors a secret passion for a woman he thinks he can never have—but fate has a way of bringing about the impossible. Read on for an excerpt...

Devices & Desires: Excerpt

Available in January 2016

Heap on more wood!—the wind is chill;
But let it whistle as it will,
We'll keep our Christmas merry still.
—Sir Walter Scott, Marmion

Yorkshire, December 1880

"GOOD GOD, are your brothers *still* arguing?" Sir Anthony Stirling demanded of his godson. "That billiards match was more than two hours ago!"

"That makes no difference, unfortunately," Lord Gervase Lyons replied. "You've heard of fellows who don't know when they're beaten? Well, that's Hal. And then there's Reg, who never knows when he's won. They'll be arguing every stroke until the Last Trump has sounded— or until my lady mother has found other employment for them."

"The latter appears a distinct possibility. I believe she intends to have them oversee the raising and decoration of the Christmas tree."

"On which they will no doubt argue the placement of every ornament and strand of tinsel," Gervase said dryly. "Having no desire to subject myself to that, I thought it best to retire to the library with you before Mother enlisted my services as well."

"Very politic of you," Sir Anthony remarked. "And it will give us some time to discuss your future in private, will it not?"

Gervase smiled. "I knew I liked you best of all my godfathers, sir."

Sir Anthony raised an eyebrow. "As I am your *only* godfather, that compliment holds rather less water than it might, my boy!"

Gervase's smile broadened into a grin. They understood each other very well, he and Sir Anthony, and always had. "But enough, I hope, to grant me a full hearing?"

For answer, his godfather sank down upon one of the padded leather armchairs by the fire, gesturing to Gervase to take the one opposite. "So, how old are you now —twenty?"

"Twenty in September, sir."

"And flourishing at Oxford?"

"My tutor believes so, yes." Indeed, Gervase's tutor cherished hopes that he'd earn a First next year, when Final Schools were held. Gervase himself did rather more than hope: First-class honors were firmly in his sights, and barring an unforeseen disaster, he meant to have them.

"And your father is no closer to making a clergyman of you than he was two years ago?"

Gervase shuddered. "God forbid, sir—if you'll pardon the expression!"

"Consider it pardoned." Sir Anthony's shrewd grey eyes regarded him appraisingly. "Well, then, I assume you have another plan for your future?" *You wouldn't be your parents' son if you didn't* was the unspoken implication.

"Yes, I mean to study law, actually."

"The law, is it? Well, there's no disgrace in such a career. Indeed, I think you would make a very creditable barrister—and perhaps, in due course, a Queen's Counsel."

"Thank you, sir, but you see—I don't wish to be a *barrister*." Gervase took a breath. "I intend to become a solicitor instead."

"A solicitor?" Sir Anthony's brows rose. "A barrister would be far more prestigious—"

"I'm the son of a duke," Gervase pointed out. "I should think that sufficiently prestigious for anyone. You see, sir, I've thought this through quite thoroughly," he continued in his most persuasive tone. "There may be more... cachet in being a barrister, but a solicitor wields just as much influence—and possibly more power. A barrister, however skilled, must still depend upon a solicitor for employment, especially during the early stages of his career. A barrister must depend upon a solicitor for *payment*—and that, I think, I should find intolerable." He paused, searching Sir Anthony's face. "I trust I need not explain why—to *you*, of all people."

"Indeed." His godfather eyed him intently. "Does your father know of your plans?"

"Not just yet, sir." Gervase's mouth crooked. "I am fortifying myself for just such an event. I expect it to be quite... cataclysmic."

"Very prudent. He's had his plans for you rather set in stone these last five or six years."

"I'm well aware of that." *And if he'd taken as much time to get to know me as he did hatching his precious scheme, perhaps he would have understood why it could never work.* "But

I wish to be my own man—not spend my life as the Duke of Whitborough's."

The very thought chilled him. A tame cleric dwelling in his father's living, beneath his father's eye—and thumb—for the rest of his life. It didn't bear thinking of. As the heir, Hal might have to remain close, but Gervase would be damned if he'd follow his brother's example.

"Hmm." Sir Anthony drummed his fingers on the chair's armrest. "If you'll permit me to play devil's advocate for a moment, your father might not be *altogether* displeased to learn of your plans. Especially if you plead your case as articulately as you have for me."

Gervase stifled a sigh. "With respect, sir, unless His Grace can convince himself that this was all *his* idea, I expect him to be very displeased indeed."

"And your mother? Have you apprised her of what you intend?"

"Mother has known since last summer that I won't enter the Church. She is surprisingly calm about it."

"Sensible woman," Sir Anthony approved. "She knows a true vocation when she sees one—or, in your case, *doesn't* see one."

"That could be." It was likewise true, Gervase reflected, that the Duchess of Whitborough tended to be less overbearing than her husband—at least when it came to her younger children. Reg, the heir to her French properties, was her favorite, and she guarded *his* rights jealously.

But that was an old grievance, with which he'd come to terms years ago. It would suffice, for now, that his mother would not oppose his plans. Indeed, she might even support them, if only because she thought it salutary for his father *not* to have his own way all the time!

"You'll need someone to take you on as an apprentice," his godfather mused aloud. "Even with a university degree, you'll have to put in several years as an articled clerk."

Gervase did his best to quell his rising excitement. "I'm not afraid of hard work, sir."

Sir Anthony nodded acknowledgment. "Which is why I hold out every hope of your succeeding in this endeavor. I'll tell you what, my boy—once the New Year begins, I shall ask among my acquaintances if they know of any solicitors who'd be willing to take you on, once you're finished at Oxford."

"Thank you, sir!" Gervase said fervently.

"And when the time comes to speak to your father, I will support you then as well."

Gervase exhaled, almost giddy with relief. "Thank you," he said again. "Truly, sir, I could hardly ask for anything more."

Sir Anthony gave him one of the rare smiles that transformed his rather saturnine face. "You're a likely young man, Gervase. The cleverest in a clever family, I shouldn't wonder. Are you *sure* you don't wish to be a barrister? You argue most eloquently on your own behalf."

Gervase smiled. "Quite certain, sir. But I am flattered that you think me eloquent."

"You should go far, with that tongue and those wits," Sir Anthony predicted, leaning back in his armchair and stifling a yawn. "Pardon me, dear boy! When one gets to be my age, a nap in the afternoon becomes less of an indulgence than a necessity."

"Then I'll leave you to your rest." Gervase rose from his chair. "And thank you again for your support, and for —well, for listening, I suppose."

His godfather smiled, his eyes already closing. "I find it refreshing to talk to someone who knows exactly what he wants. So many young people *don't*, nowadays." He yawned again, sinking deeper into the cushions. "Very far indeed," he murmured, not even stirring as Gervase solicitously draped an afghan over him before stealing from the library.

Easing the door closed behind him, Gervase made his way along the passage, his spirits considerably lighter than before. No doubt there'd be a reckoning when he finally revealed his future plans to his father—the Duke of Whitborough was nothing if not autocratic—but with Sir Anthony's support and his mother's lack of opposition, he stood a good chance of prevailing.

A burst of laughter issued from the Great Hall, further down the passage. Laughter, followed by a snatch of song: "*A-wassail, a-wassail, all over the town—*"

His younger sisters, Elaine and Juliana, the most musical of the family. In spite of his earlier reluctance, Gervase found himself drifting towards the source of that sound. Denforth Castle, *en fête* for the Christmas holidays. For all his cynicism, that was still a sight worth seeing.

The carol broke off amidst more laughter, as his sisters debated the next lines. And Gervase could hear the hum of other conversations now, a medley of different voices, including his mother's rich, throaty contralto and his father's deep, authoritative baritone. Their Graces of Whitborough, presiding over their considerable brood.

Pausing outside the doorway, Gervase peered into the room. From this distance, he could study his family more objectively... like the outsider and observer he so often felt himself to be. His gaze rested first upon his mother, who never ceased to command with her very presence: Helene de Sevigny-Lyons, regal and still beautiful, in spite of or perhaps even because of the silver threading her black hair like tinsel. Swathed in a crimson velvet cloak—his mother loved rich colors—she stood in the center of the Hall supervising the decoration of their Christmas tree, fully seven feet high this year.

And where Her Grace was, His Grace could not be far away—at least, not at Christmas. The duke and duchess fought as fiercely as they loved, but somehow, that ceased to matter once the snows began to fall. And there was Father, Gervase observed, casual as a country squire in tweeds and riding boots, his tawny hair rumpled and standing on end, striding about to examine the tree from every angle and occasionally countermand his wife's orders. The servants, long accustomed to such dissension, worked stolidly on.

And speaking of dissension, there were his two older brothers, ostentatiously ignoring each other on opposite sides of the tree... though Gervase would have wagered the contents of his library that they were darting hissing asides criticizing each other's handiwork when they thought their parents weren't listening. Young Harold, called "Hal"—his father's heir and namesake—must have got off a particularly stinging rejoinder, to judge from his smug expression... and Reg's fulminating one. But then Hal was one of fortune's darlings, supremely confident of his charms and secure in his position as firstborn.

Insufferably complacent, Reg would have said, jutting

out that masterful chin of his. And Gervase might have agreed, had he not found Reg equally insufferable in his way. Aggressive, competitive, determined to prove himself the best at every masculine endeavor... the army should provide sufficient outlet for *his* energies, Gervase mused. Reg would be joining a cavalry regiment in the New Year—a natural choice, as he rode like a centaur.

With something like relief, Gervase sought out his sisters and found them more peaceably engaged at the other end of the Hall, sorting through baskets overflowing with holly, ivy, and mistletoe. Madeline, Hal's twin but dark-haired like their mother, her slim form just beginning to ripen with her impending motherhood, was directing the placement of greenery, while her husband, Hugo, Viscount Saxby, hovered protectively. And there was Elaine, golden and cheerful as a sunbeam, starting up another carol, accompanied by vivacious, flame-haired Juliana, still in the schoolroom but promising to equal her sisters in beauty and charm.

A small dark shadow wandered disconsolately between his elders. Jason, the youngest at almost eleven—and probably feeling his lack of importance very much at this moment. The changeling, Gervase had heard his little brother called, which he privately thought was unfair as the boy's coloring was actually quite similar to their mother's, and as for his height... well, Jason had some growing yet to do, and not everyone could be as tall as Hal or Reg. Gervase was a good two to three inches shorter than they, with grey eyes rather than blue and hair more bronze than gold. Given the choice, he'd have preferred to be dramatically dark like Jason.

There'd be whining in a moment, Gervase thought, watching the frown developing between the boy's brows, the pout forming on his lips. Or at the very least, a complaint of how bored he was. But before either could take place, the duke strode over to rumple his youngest son's hair, then swept him up—all smiles now—into his arms with easy affection.

He spoiled that boy shamelessly, Gervase thought. But it was Christmas, and what was the harm with a bit of spoiling then? And the duchess had always found dealing with her youngest child difficult—for reasons that none of the family ever openly discussed.

Family... for better and for worse, these people defined him, Gervase realized. Not in his entirety, perhaps, but he would not be the person he was without them. And if he wanted, he could walk right into the room now, and become a part of the scene. Instantly recognized and accepted, as a son of the house should be. And his parents would smile at him, his sisters would invite him to help sort greenery, and his brothers might even take a moment from their ongoing competition to ask his opinion on some Christmas tree-related matter.

He took a step toward that laughing family group— and then stopped dead in his tracks.

She passed before the doorway, her hands full of ivy, their glossy leaves the same color as the dress that clung so delightfully to her newly mature figure: just eighteen and set to make her debut in spring. Richly waving hair the color of ripe chestnuts, velvety brown eyes like a doe's... eyes doubtless fixed on handsome, golden Hal— as was only right, fitting, and proper.

And Gervase found his feet moving, seemingly of their own volition, carrying him past the Hall and towards the staircase leading up to his chamber—and some much-needed privacy. He'd come back later, he told himself. When he felt more confident of his ability to conceal these highly inconvenient and inappropriate yearnings.

Someone who knows what he wants, his godfather had called him. But what good did *that* do, he wondered bleakly, when you had no hope of ever getting it? He mounted the stairs, doing his best to block out the sounds of laughter and song behind him. And *her* voice most of all.

Everyone in the family knew, to some extent, how much Reg coveted the dukedom and Hal's place as firstborn.

No one knew—no one would ever know, if Gervase had anything to say about it—how much *he* coveted Hal's fiancée.

The Story Behind The Story

THE ADVENT OF LADY MADELINE represents a series of firsts for me, as much as it does for my hero, Hugo. Never before have I written a prequel. Never before have I written back-to-front in a series. And never before have I written—essentially—a "jock hero."

I can pinpoint almost the exact moment when **The Lyons Pride** was "born": in December 2012, while I was writing a guest blog to promote my debut novel, *Waltz with a Stranger*. The topic was families in romance, and while discussing the various clans I'd encountered as a reader of the genre, I suddenly flashed on a moment in *The Lion in Winter*, one of my favorite films of all time. Specifically, the moment where Eleanor of Aquitaine (Katharine Hepburn) drives her husband, Henry II (Peter O'Toole), literally screaming from the room, then slides down a wall, murmuring, "Well, what family doesn't have its ups and downs?"

Few would argue that the Angevin Plantagenets were among the most dysfunctional families in history, which was surely exacerbated by how much power and influence they wielded not only in England but in France as well. The idea took hold of me: who might these people be in another time and place, in a slightly different set of circumstances? Would their destinies play out in the exact same tragic way? Or would it be possible for these contentious, competitive, too-clever-for-their-own-good people to win happier endings than their historical counterparts did?

Reimagining historical characters and events in a more modern context isn't exactly new. Susan Howatch updated the Angevins' story to Edwardian Cornwall and beyond in *Penmarric*, and retained most of its tragic elements. And *Empire*, a new television series on FOX, transfers it to the present day and uses the hip-hop music industry as a background. I have yet to see a single episode of *Empire*, but the reported parallels amuse me—and so does the family's surname, which differs by one letter from my own choice. Pure coincidence, I assure you!

I chose late Victorian England as the setting for my series, approximately 700 years after *The Lion in Winter*, which takes place in 1183. And Yorkshire, an appropriately wild, rugged location that evokes memories for me of the Brontës, *The Secret Garden*, and Richard III. I started writing the first book—*Devices & Desires*—in mid-2013, and finished in late 2014, after a difficult stretch of real life that I've referred to as "The Summer of Suck." I was relieved to have completed it against what sometimes felt like impossible odds, cautiously pleased with the result, and prepared to take a short hiatus to concentrate on other projects while letting nascent ideas percolate for the next novel in the series.

Except then the hero's older sister, Madeline, tapped me on the shoulder and insisted that I tell *her* story, which takes place almost a decade before *Devices & Desires*. Now, as a general rule, my muse prefers generating sequels. Prequels can be such disobliging things, only showing their significance after the fact, to which an exasperated author might exclaim: "Where were you *before* I started writing Book One? And why should I tie myself in knots trying to fit you into the timeline *now*? Okay, fine—here's a flashback. Now go away, and stop bothering me."

Except when they won't, which turned out to be the case here. In retrospect, I shouldn't really have been surprised: Madeline is a Lyons, after all, and as imperious as the rest of the family. Once I bowed to the inevitable, however, I found myself enjoying the experience of developing her story. For one thing, I had more latitude with Madeline than I did with her parents and brothers. Henry and Eleanor's daughters were all sent away as children to make foreign marriages of alliance. (Matilda—Madeline's historical counterpart—was married at eleven to Henry, Duke of Saxony, who was almost thirty years older.) That was less likely to happen in the time I'd chosen, so I could develop her as an adult character.

I could also flesh out the love story and make Madeline's husband, Hugo, more of a person too. I'd established him in *Devices & Desires* as an amiable, easygoing, aristocratic sportsman—a bit of a departure for me, since my heroes tend to be intellectuals, artists, or hard-working professional men. What might Madeline see in a man who, on the surface, was so different from her and from the males who surrounded her while she was growing up? What attracts an artist to "a jock"—beyond the physical appeal, of course!

The surprise for me was that I became as fond of the good-natured, unassuming Hugo as I was of Madeline. Kindness is one of the most appealing traits a character can possess, and Hugo had it in spades. Plus, writing from his point-of-view allowed me a new perspective on the Lyons family, as a whole. Like the reader, Hugo is meeting them for the first time, as an outsider. He doesn't yet know what makes them tick... but he's about to find out.

So when it comes to writing prequels, I have learned to "never say never." Because sometimes an experience that you've previously rejected out of hand turns out to be more fun than you can possibly imagine!

As for Madeline and Hugo, they'll be back! As supporting characters and, perhaps, someday as leads in another story. **The Lyons Pride** will likely keep me busy for some time to come—and I wouldn't have it any other way.

Acknowledgments

I OWE MORE than I can possibly say to the following:

My betas, especially Angela, for pushing me across the finish line every time I start this race.

Kim Killion of The Killion Group for designing a beautiful cover that exceeded all my expectations and made me determined to write a story that lived up to it.

Dawn Charles of BookGraphics.Net for the Blue Castle logo, which makes me feel like a pro whenever I look at it.

The community of self-published and hybrid authors, who share their experience and advice so generously.

My family, for their support and their faith in me.

My readers, who remind me every day that the stories are what matter.

About the Author

Pamela Sherwood is an avid reader of multiple genres (horror excepted) and aspires to be a prolific writer of multiple genres (again, horror excepted). In a previous life, she earned a doctorate in English literature, specializing in the Romantic and Victorian periods, and taught college-level literature and writing courses. At present, she writes historical romance and fantasy. Her books have received starred reviews in *Booklist* and *Library Journal*, and *Waltz with a Stranger*, her debut novel, won the Laurel Wreath Award for Best Historical Romance in 2013. She recently published her first work of fantasy, *Awakened and Other Enchanted Tales*. Pamela lives with her family in Southern California, where she continues to read voraciously, spin plots, and straddle genres to tell the kind of stories she loves.

Visit her on the web at http://pamelasherwood.com, facebook.com/PamelaSherwoodAuthor, and twitter.com/#!/pamela_sherwood

Also by Pamela Sherwood

The Lyons Pride
The Advent of Lady Madeline
Devices & Desires
Twelfth Night
Epiphany
Intimate Delights (collection)
A Lyons in Winter (box set)
A Bride by Michaelmas (forthcoming)
Women & Wine (forthcoming)

The Heiress Series
Waltz with a Stranger
A Scandal in Newport
A Song at Twilight
A Wedding in Cornwall
The Heiress Brides (collection)

Short Story Collections
Awakened and Other Enchanted Tales